SNOWBOUND SURPRISE FOR THE BILLIONAIRE

SNOWBOUND SURPRISE FOR THE BILLIONAIRE

BY
MICHELLE DOUGLAS

First published in Great Britain 2014
by Mills & Boon, an imprint of Harlequin (UK) Limited,
Large Print edition 2015
Eton House, 18-24 Paradise Road,
Richmond, Surrey, TW9 1SR

© 2014 Michelle Douglas

ISBN: 978-0-263-25622-2

Harlequin (UK) Limited's policy is to use papers that
are natural, renewable and recyclable products and made
from wood grown in sustainable forests. The logging
and manufacturing processes conform to the legal
environmental regulations of the country of origin.

Printed and bound in Great Britain
by CPI Antony Rowe, Chippenham, Wiltshire

To my Romance Authors' Google Group—
thank you, ladies, for your wisdom,
your support and your friendship.

CHAPTER ONE

ADDIE SAUNTERED DOWN to Bruce Augustus's pen, keeping her head high and her limbs loose while her lungs cramped and her eyes stung. There was probably no one watching her, but just in case.

She rounded the corner of the pen where the galvanised iron shelter finally hid her from the homestead. Pressing the back of her hand to her mouth, she swung herself over the fence, upturned the feed bin, collapsed down onto it and finally gave way to the sobs that raked through her.

The huge Hereford stud bull—ex-stud bull, he'd been retired for a few years now—nuzzled her ear. She leant forward, wrapped her arms around him and cried into his massive shoulder. He just stood there, nuzzling her and giving off animal warmth and a measure of comfort. Eventually though he snorted and stamped a foot and Addie knew it was time to pull herself together.

She eased away to rest back against the wooden palings behind and scrubbed her hands down her face. 'Sorry, Bruce Augustus, what a big cry baby you must think me.'

He lowered his head to her lap and she scratched her hands up his nose and around his ears the way he loved. He groaned and rocked into her slightly, but she wasn't afraid. He might be twelve hundred pounds of brute animal strength, but he'd never hurt her. They'd been hanging out since she was eight years old. She'd cried with him when her mother had died two years ago. She'd cried with him when her father had died four months ago.

And she'd cried with him when her best friend, Robbie, had died.

She closed her eyes. Her head dropped. Robbie.

Finally she'd thought she'd be free to keep her promise to Robbie, had practically tasted the freedom of it on her tongue. But no. Flynn Mather in his perfect suit and with his perfectly cool—some might say cold—business manner had just presented his contract to them all. A contract with an insidious heartbreaking condition.

She stood and turned to survey the fields that rolled away in front of her, at the ranges way off to her right, and at the stands of ancient gum trees. She propped her arms on the fence and rested her chin on them. In early December in the Central

West Tablelands of New South Wales, the grass was golden, the sky was an unending blue and the sun was fierce. She dashed away the perspiration that pricked her brow. 'How long do you think Robbie would've given me to fulfil my promise, Bruce Augustus?'

Of course he didn't answer.

She made herself smile—might as well practise out here where no one could see her. 'The good news is we've found a buyer for Lorna Lee's.'

A sigh juddered out of her. She and two of her neighbours had joined forces to sell their properties as a job lot. Frank and Jeannie were well past retirement age, while Eric and Lucy were spending so much time in Sydney for four-year-old Colin's treatment their place was in danger of falling into wrack and ruin. Addie and her father had helped out all they could, but when her father had died it was all Addie could do to keep on top of things here at Lorna Lee's. One person really did make that much of a difference. And when that person was gone…

She stared up at the sky and breathed deeply. No more crying today. Besides, she'd already cried buckets for her father.

She leant a shoulder against Bruce's bulk. 'So

our gamble paid off.' Putting the three properties together for sale had made it a more attractive venture for at least one buyer. Flynn Mather. 'Your new owner is a hotshot businessman. He also has a cattle station in Queensland Channel country—huge apparently.'

Bruce Augustus snorted.

'Don't be like that. He knows his stuff. Says he wants to diversify his portfolio.' She snorted then too. Who actually spoke like that? 'And he plans to expand the breeding programme here.' She practised another smile. 'That's good news, huh?'

The bull merely swished his tail, dislodging several enormous horseflies.

'We have a buyer. I should be over the moon.' She gripped the wooden paling until her knuckles turned white. 'But you know what I'd really like to do?' She glared at gorgeous golden fields. 'I'd like to take that contract and tell him to shove it where the sun don't shine.'

Bruce Augustus shook his head, dislodging the horse flies from his face. Addie grabbed the plastic swatter she'd hung on a nail by the fence and splattered both flies in one practised swat. Bruce Augustus didn't even flinch. 'That's what I'd like to do with Flynn Mather's contract.'

Two years! He'd demanded she stay here for *two whole years* to oversee the breeding programme and to train someone up. He'd made it a condition of that rotten contract.

A well of something dark and suffocating rose inside her. She swallowed. 'That means spending Christmas here.' She straightened and scowled. 'No way! I'm not some indentured servant. I'm allowed to leave. I'm *not* spending Christmas on the farm!'

The anger drained out of her. She collapsed back onto the feed bin. 'How am I going to stand it, Bruce? How am I going to cope with two more years in this godforsaken place, treading water while everyone else gets to live their dreams? When am I going to be allowed to follow my dreams?'

Robbie hadn't lived her dreams. She'd died before her time. Leukaemia. But Addie had promised to live them for her. Dreams of travel. Dreams of adventure in exotic lands. They'd marked out routes on maps, made lists of must-see places, had kept records of not-to-be missed sights. They'd planned out in minute detail how they'd office temp in London, work the ski lifts in Switzerland and be barmaids in German beer halls. They'd teach English as a second language in Japan and save enough money to go trekking in Nepal. They'd even taken

French and Japanese in high school as preparation. Robbie had become too sick to finish her studies, but on her better days Addie had done what she could to catch her up with the French—Robbie's favourite.

But now…

But now Robbie was dead and Addie was stuck on the farm for another two years.

She dropped her head to her hands. 'You know what I'm afraid of, Bruce Augustus? That I'll never leave this place, that I'll get trapped here, and that I won't even have one adventure. I'm scared that I'll get so lonely Aaron Frey will wear me down and before I know it I'll find myself married with four kids and hating my life.' And if that proved the case then Robbie should've been the one to live. Not her.

She glared at a bale of straw. 'All I want is to see the world. Other than you, Bruce Augustus, there's nothing I'll miss from this place.' Not now that her parents were dead. 'Of course I'd come back to see you, and Molly Margaret and Roger Claudius and Donald Erasmus too. Goes without saying.'

She tried to battle the weariness that descended over her, the depression that had hovered over her since her father's death.

'If it were just me I'd tell Mather to take a hike, but it isn't just me.' She stood and dusted off her hands. Jeannie and Frank deserved to retire in comfort and ease. Little Colin with Down's syndrome and all the associated health challenges that presented deserved a chance for as full a life as he could have, and his parents deserved the chance to focus on him without the worries of a farm plaguing them.

'You're right, Bruce. It's time to time stop whining and suck it up.' She couldn't turn Flynn Mather away. Given the current economic climate there were no guarantees another buyer could be found—certainly not one willing to pay the asking price. Flynn hadn't quibbled over that.

She let out a long slow breath. 'The pity party's over. I have a contract to sign.' She kissed Bruce Augustus's nose, vaulted the fence and set off towards the main house—chin up and shoulders back, whistling as if she didn't have a care in the world.

Flynn watched Adelaide Ramsey saunter back towards the house. He rested his head against the corrugated iron of the shed and swore softly. Damn it all to hell!

Looking at her now, nobody would guess all she'd confided to her bull.

He moved around to glance in the pen. The bull eyeballed him and his head lowered. 'Yeah, yeah, I'm the villain of the piece.'

One ear flicked forward. 'The problem is, Bruce Augustus—' What a name! '—I have plans for this place, big plans, and your mistress knows her stuff. She knows this place better than anyone on the planet.' Her expertise would be key to his success here.

The bull snorted and Flynn shook his head. 'I can't believe I'm talking to a bull.'

When am I going to be allowed to follow my dreams?

It had been a cry from the heart. His chest tightened as if in a vice. He couldn't afford to lose Addie and her expertise, but he didn't traffic in other people's misery either. He didn't want her to feel trapped here. He scratched a hand through his hair. Was there something he could offer her to soften her disappointment, something that would make her want to stay?

His phone rang and the bull's head reared back. Flynn knew enough about bulls to know it was time to beat a hasty retreat. He glanced at the caller

ID as he moved away and lifted the phone to his ear with a grim smile, turning his steps towards the Ramsey homestead—his homestead once she signed the contract.

'Hans, hello,' he said to the lawyer.

'Good news, Herr Mather. The will is due to go through probate in two weeks' time. After that the premises you're interested in will go on the market and you can bid for them.'

His heart beat hard. His smile turned grimmer. 'Excellent news.'

'I take it you will be in Munich for Christmas?'

'Correct.'

I'm not spending Christmas on the farm!

Flynn straightened. 'We'll confer again soon.'

All I want is to see the world?

He snapped his cell phone shut and vaulted up the stairs to the veranda. Voices emerged from the front room.

'Look, lass, we know you want to leave this place too. We can wait to see if another buyer shows interest.'

'Don't be silly, Frank.' That was Adelaide. He recognised the low, rich tones of her voice. 'Who knows if another buyer could be found, let alone when?'

'Lucy, Colin and I need to leave as soon as it can be arranged. I know that sounds hard and I'm sorry, but...'

That was Eric Seymour. Flynn didn't like the other man, but then he didn't have a seriously ill child in need of surgery either. In the same circumstances he'd probably be just as ruthless.

You are that ruthless.

He pushed that thought away.

Eric spoke again. 'If you decide to turn down Mather's offer, Addie, then I'm going to insist you buy out my farm like you once offered to. I can't wait any longer.'

The bank would lend her the necessary money. Flynn didn't doubt that for a moment. But it'd put her in debt up to her eyeballs.

'Don't get your knickers in a knot, Eric. I intend to sign the contract. All of us here understand your situation and we don't want to delay you a moment longer than necessary. We want the very best for Colin too. We're behind you a hundred per cent.'

'Lucy and I know that.'

'But, love,' Jeannie started.

Time to step in. Flynn strode across the veranda, making sure his footfalls echoed. He entered the front parlour. 'I'm sorry. I had a couple of business calls to make.'

Addie opened her mouth, but he continued before she could speak. 'I get the distinct impression, Ms Ramsey, that you're not exactly thrilled with the prospect of being bound to Lorna Lee's for the next two years?'

'Addie,' she said for what must've been the sixth time that day. 'Please call me Addie.' Although she tried to hide it, her eyes lit up in a way that had his heart beating hard. 'Have you changed your mind about that condition?'

'No.'

Her face fell.

His heart burned. 'Obviously the offer of a very generous salary package hasn't quite overcome your objections.'

'Oh, I…' She trailed off. She attempted what he suspected was a smile but it looked more like a grimace.

He held himself tall and taut. 'So I've been mulling over some other bonuses that you might find more tempting and will, therefore, lead you to signing the contract without hesitation.'

She glanced at her neighbours, opened her mouth and then closed it again. 'Oh?'

'I want to make it clear that you won't be confined here. It's not necessary that you spend the entirety of the next seven hundred and thirty days chained to the farm.'

Her shoulders sagged.

'You will be entitled to four weeks of annual leave a year. Would an annual business-class airfare to anywhere in the world, return of course, sweeten the deal for you? I will offer it for every year you work for me—whether that's the two years stipulated in the contract or longer if you decide to stay on.'

Her jaw dropped. Her eyes widened, and he suddenly realised they were the most startling shade of brown he'd ever seen—warm amber with copper highlights that flared as if embers in a hearth fire. He stared, caught up in trying to define their colour even more precisely as Frank, Jeannie and Eric all started talking over the top of each other. Addie's expression snapped closed as if the noise had brought her back to herself and he suddenly discovered he couldn't read her expression at all.

She laughed and clapped her hands, and he was suddenly reminded of the way she'd whistled as she'd walked away from Bruce Augustus's pen.

'Where do I sign? Mr Mather, you have yourself a deal.'

'Flynn,' he found himself saying. 'Call me Flynn.'

'I have another offer slash request to run past you as well.'

She blinked. How on earth hadn't he noticed those eyes earlier? 'Which is?'

'I have business in Munich later this month.'

'Munich? Munich in Germany?' She rubbed a hand against her chest as if to ease an ache there.

'The same. The business that calls me there is moving more quickly than originally anticipated so I find myself in a bit of a bind. I promised my PA that she could have several weeks' leave over Christmas, you see?'

'Your PA?' Addie said.

He could tell she only asked from politeness and had no idea where he was going with this. He straightened. 'Would you consider accompanying me to Munich and acting as my assistant for three or four weeks?'

Her jaw dropped.

She wanted to say yes; he could see that.

She hauled her jaw back into place. 'Why would you offer that position to me? I've never been a secretary before or even an office assistant.'

'You keep all of the farm's financial records. You put together the marketing and PR documents. You have a filing system that's in good order. I don't doubt you have the skills I need.' To be perfectly frank what he needed was a lackey, an offsider, someone who would jump to do his bidding when it was asked of them.

'Germany, love,' Jeannie breathed. 'What an adventure.'

Addie bit her lip and peered at him through narrowed eyes. 'I expect I'd be on call twenty-four seven?'

'Then you'd expect wrong. You'll have plenty of time for sightseeing.'

Why didn't she just say yes? Or wasn't she used to good fortune dropping into her lap? If she didn't want it there were at least five other people ready to jump at the chance to take her place.

'I do have an ulterior motive,' he said. 'I want to learn all I can about Lorna Lee's breeding programme. That means I'll be spending a significant amount of time here over the course of the next two years. Once I'm up to speed I'll know what changes to implement, where an injection of capital will be most beneficial...where to expand operations.'

She frowned. 'Changes?'

He almost laughed at her proprietorial tone. 'Changes,' he repeated, keeping his voice firm. Once she signed the contract, and after the obligatory cooling-off period, the farm would be his. 'As we'll be working closely together over the next few months, Addie—' he used the diminutive of her Christian name deliberately '—the sooner we get to know each other, the better.'

She stared at him as if seeing him for the first time. 'You actually mean to be hands-on at Lorna Lee's?'

It wasn't his usual practice, but he'd taken one look at this property and a knot inside him had unravelled. Lorna Lee's might, in fact, become his home base. 'That's right.'

She shook herself. 'Okay, well, first things first. Let's deal with the contract.'

That suited him just fine. He added in a clause outlining her new bonus before scrawling his signature at the bottom and moving across to the other side of the room.

Eric signed first. Frank and Jeannie added their signatures next. Jeannie held the pen out to Addie. She cast her eyes around the room once before taking the pen and adding her signature in turn.

Deal done.

Eric slapped his hat to his head. 'I'm off to tell Lucy the good news. We plan to be gone just after Christmas.'

Both Frank and Addie nodded.

Jeannie patted Addie's arm. 'I'm overdue for my nanna nap, love. We'll see you later. Why don't you come over for dinner?'

'Okay, thanks.'

Everyone left and as soon as the door closed behind them Addie's shoulders slumped. Flynn swallowed, hoping she wasn't going to cry again. He cleared his throat and her chin shot up and her shoulders pushed back. She swung around to face him. 'You mentioned you wanted another tour of the property today too, right?'

He nodded. He'd specifically requested that she accompany him.

'Would you like that tour now or do you have more business calls to make?'

She glanced at the cell phone he held. He stowed it away. Before he'd heard what he had at Bruce Augustus's pen, he'd thought he had her pegged—a no-nonsense, competent country girl.

When am I going to be allowed to follow my dreams?

Other than a desire to see the world, what were her dreams?

He shook off the thought. Her dreams were none of his concern. All he wanted was to reconcile her to the contract she'd just signed. Once that was done she'd be a model employee. A problem solved. Then he could move forward with his plans for the place.

'Now would be good if that suits you. I'd like to get changed first, though.'

She directed him to a spare bedroom, where he pulled on jeans, a T-shirt and riding boots.

When he returned, Addie glanced around and then her jaw dropped.

He frowned. 'What?'

'I just…' She reddened. She dragged her gaze away. It returned a few seconds later. 'I know you have a station in Channel country and all, but… heck, Flynn. Now you look like someone who could put in an honest day's work.'

He stiffened. 'You don't believe honest work can be achieved in a suit?'

'Sure it can.' She didn't sound convinced. 'Just not the kind of work we do around here.'

Before he could quiz her further she led him out of the front door. 'As you probably recall from the deeds to the properties, the Seymour farm extends from the boundary fence to the right of Lorna Lee's while Frank and Jeannie's extends in a wedge shape behind.'

He nodded. The individual farms shared an access road from the highway that led into the township of Mudgee, which was roughly twenty minutes away. There was another property to the eastern boundary of Lorna Lee's. If it ever came onto the market he'd snap it up as well. But, at the moment, all up, he'd just acquired seven hundred acres of prime beef country.

'The three individual farmhouses are of a similar size. I expect you'd like one of them as your home base if you mean to spend a lot of time here. Which one should I organise for you?'

He blinked. At the moment she was certainly no-nonsense and practical. 'I want you to remain at the homestead here. You're familiar with it and it'll only create an unnecessary distraction to move you from it. I'll base myself at the Marsh place.' Frank and Jeannie's. It was closer to Lorna Lee's than the Seymour homestead. 'Next year I'll hire a foreman and a housekeeper—a husband and wife team ideally, so keep your ear to the ground.

They can have the Seymour house. There are workers' quarters if the need arises.'

He didn't want her to move out of her family home? Addie couldn't have said why, but a knot of tension eased out of her.

They talked business as they made their way over to the massive machinery shed. There'd been an itemised account of all farm equipment attached to the contract, but she went over it all again.

Because he wanted her to.

Because he was now her boss.

And because he'd held the promise of Munich out to her like a treasure of epic proportions and it shimmered in her mind like a mirage.

She glanced at his boots. 'Were you hoping to ride around the property?'

'I'd appreciate it if that could be arranged.'

'Saddle up Banjo and Blossom,' she told Logan, her lone farmhand. Correction. Flynn's farmhand. She swung to him, hands on hips. 'You're wearing riding boots and you own a cattle station. I'm assuming you know your way around a horse.'

The man finally smiled. She'd started to think he didn't know how, that he was a machine—all cold, clinical efficiency.

'You assume right.'

For no reason at all her heart started thundering in her chest. She had to swallow before she could speak. 'I gave you a comprehensive tour of Lorna Lee's two weeks ago and I know both Frank and Eric did the same at their places. You and your people went over it all with a fine-tooth comb.' What was he actually hoping she'd show him?

'We studied points of interest—dams, fences, sheds and equipment, irrigation systems—but nothing beats getting to know the layout of the land like riding it.'

Question answered.

She rubbed the nape of her neck and tried to get her breathing back under control. It was probably the release of tension from having finally signed, but Flynn looked different in jeans and boots. He looked… She rolled her shoulders. Hot. As in *adventure* hot.

She shook her head. Crazy thought. Who cared what he looked like? She just wanted him to look after the farm, develop it to its full potential, while hoping he wasn't an absolute tyrant to work for. All of those things trumped *hot* any day.

Logan brought out the steeds and Flynn moved to take the reins from him. She selected an Akubra from a peg—an old one of her father's that had her swallowing back a lump—and handed it to him, before slapping her own hat to her head. The afternoon had lengthened but the sun would still be warm.

She glanced at the two horses. She'd been going to take Blossom, but… She glanced back at Flynn.

He gazed back steadily. 'What?'

'What are you in the mood for? An easy, relaxed ride or—' she grinned '—something more challenging?'

'Addie, something you ought to know about me from the get go is that I'll always choose challenging.'

Right. 'Then Blossom is all yours.' She indicated the grey. 'I'll take Banjo.'

'Leg up?' he offered.

If it'd been Logan, she'd have accepted. If Flynn had been in his business suit she'd have probably accepted—just to test him. But the large maleness of him as he moved in closer, all of the muscled strength clearly outlined in jeans and T-shirt, had her baulking. 'No, thank you.'

She slipped her foot into the stirrup and swung herself up into the saddle. Before she could be snarky and ask if he'd like a leg up, he'd done the same. Effortlessly. The big grey danced but Flynn handled him with ease. Perfectly.

She bit back a sigh. She suspected Flynn was one of those people who did everything perfectly.

He raised an eyebrow. 'Pass muster?'

'You'll do,' she muttered, turning her horse and hoping the movement hid the flare of colour that heated her cheeks.

She led the way out of the home paddock and then finally looked at him again. 'What in particular would you like to see?' Was there a particular herd he wanted to look over, a particular stretch of watercourse or a landscape feature?

'To be perfectly frank, Addie, there's nothing in particular I want to see. I just want to be out amongst it.'

He was tired of being cooped up. *That* she could deal with. She pointed. 'See that stand of ironbarks on the low hill over there?'

'Uh-huh.'

'Wait for me there.'

He frowned. 'Wait?'

She nodded at his steed. 'In his current mood, Blossom will leave Banjo in the dust.' And without another word she dug her heels into Banjo's sides and set off at a canter.

As predicted, within ten seconds Blossom—and Flynn—had overtaken them and pulled ahead. Addie didn't care. She gave herself up to the smooth easy motion of the canter, the cooling afternoon and the scent of sun-warmed grasses—all the gnarls inside her working themselves free.

'Better?' she asked when she reached Flynn again.

He slanted her a grin. 'How'd you know?'

'I start to feel exactly the same way when I'm cooped up for too long. There's nothing like a good gallop to ease the kinks.'

He stared at her for a long moment. She thought he meant to say something, but he evidently decided to keep it to himself.

'Munich,' she blurted out, unable to keep her thoughts in.

'What do you want to know?'

'What would my duties be?'

'A bit of office support—some word processing, accessing databases and spreadsheets, and setting up the odd meeting. If I want printing done, you'll be my go-to person. The hotel will have business facilities. There might be the odd letter to post.'

This was her and Robbie's dream job!

'But...' she bit her lip '...I don't know any German beyond *danke* and *guten Tag*.'

He raised an eyebrow. *'Auf wiedersehen?'*

Oh, right. She nodded. 'Goodbye.'

'Those phrases will serve you well enough. You'll find you won't need to know the language. Most Europeans speak perfect English.'

Wow. Still, if she did go she meant to bone up on as much conversational German as she could.

'You'll be doing a lot of fetching and carrying— Get me that file, Addie. Where's the Parker document, Addie? Ring down for coffee, will you, Addie? Where're the most recent sales figures and costing sheets? Things like that.'

That she could do. She could major in fetching and carrying. 'When are you planning to leave?'

'In a week's time.'

Oh, wow!

He frowned. 'Do you have a passport?'

'Yes.' She'd had one since she was seventeen. Robbie had wanted one, and even though by that stage it had been pointless, Robbie's parents hadn't been able to deny her anything. She'd wanted Addie to have one too. Addie had kept it up to date ever since.

'Good. Now be warned, when we work the pace

will be fast and furious, but there'll be days—lots of them, I expect—when we'll be twiddling our thumbs. Days when you'll be free to sightsee.'

It was every dream she'd ever dreamed.

She straightened, slowly, but she felt a reverberation through her entire being. There was more than one way to get off the farm. If she played this right…

'Naturally I'll cover your expenses—airfare and accommodation—along with a wage.'

A lump lodged in her throat.

'I meant what I said earlier, Addie. I want us to build a solid working relationship and I'm not the kind of man to put off the things I want. I don't see any reason why that working relationship can't start in Munich.'

If she did a great job for him, if she proved herself a brilliant personal assistant, then maybe Flynn would keep her on as his PA? She could live the life she'd always been meant to live—striding out in a suit and jet-setting around the world.

He stared at her. Eventually he pushed the brim of his hat back as if to view her all the more intently or clearly. 'Mind if I ask you something?'

'Sure.'

'Why haven't you said yes to Munich yet? I can tell you want to.'

She moistened her lips and glanced out at the horizon. 'Have you ever wanted something so badly that when you finally think it's yours you're afraid it's too good to be true?'

He was silent for a moment and then nodded. 'I know exactly how that feels.'

She believed him.

'All you have to do is say yes, Addie.'

So she said it. 'Yes.'

CHAPTER TWO

FLYNN GLANCED ACROSS at Addie, who'd started to droop. 'Are you okay?'

She shook herself upright. 'Yes, thank you.'

He raised an eyebrow.

She gritted her teeth and wriggled back in her seat. 'When can we get off this tin can?'

They'd arrived at Munich airport and were waiting for a gate to become vacant. They'd been on the ground and waiting for fifteen minutes, but he silently agreed with her. It felt more like an hour. 'Shortly, I expect, but I thought you were looking forward to flying?'

'I've flown now. It's ticked off my list,' she ground out, and then she stilled and turned those extraordinary eyes to him. 'Not that it hasn't been interesting, but I just didn't know that twenty-two hours could take so long.'

Addie's problem was that she'd been so excited when they'd first boarded the plane in Sydney she hadn't slept a wink on the nine-and-a-half-hour

leg between there and Bangkok. She'd worn herself out so much—had become so overtired—that
she'd been lucky to get two hours' sleep over the
next twelve hours.

He suspected she wasn't used to the inactivity
either. He thought back to the way they'd cantered
across the fields at Lorna Lee's and shook his head.
Overtired and climbing walls. He understood completely.

A steward's voice chimed through the sound system telling them they were taxiing to Gate Twenty-
eight and to remain in their seats. Addie blew out
a breath that made him laugh. Within twenty minutes, however, they'd cleared Customs and were
waiting by the luggage carousel. Addie eased forward in one lithe movement and hefted a bag from
the carousel as if it were a bale of hay.

He widened his stance and frowned at her. 'If
you'd pointed it out I'd have got it for you.'

She blinked at him. 'Why would you do that
when I'm more than capable?'

A laugh escaped him. 'Because I'm the big strong
man and you're the dainty personal assistant.'

One side of her mouth hooked up and her eyes
danced. 'You didn't tell me dainty was part of the
job description.' And then she moved forward,

picked his suitcase off the carousel and set it at his feet.

'Addie!'

'Fetch and carry—that was part of the job description and that I can do.'

He folded his arms. 'How'd you know it was my case? It's standard black and nondescript.'

She pointed. 'With a blue and green tartan ribbon tied to the handle.'

She'd noticed that? 'Adelaide Ramsey, I have a feeling you're going to be a handy person to have around.'

'That's the plan.'

Was it? Her earnestness puzzled him.

And then she jumped on the spot. 'Can we go and see Munich now?'

All of her weariness had fled. Her back had straightened, her eyes had brightened and she glanced about with interest. He swallowed and led the way out of the airport to the taxi stand. 'It'll take about forty minutes by cab to reach Munich proper.'

'It's so cold!'

He turned to find Addie struggling to pull her coat from her hand luggage and haul it on, her breath misting on the air. 'December in Munich,' he pointed out. 'It was always going to be cold.'

Teeth chattering, she nodded. 'I'm counting on snow.'

She spent the entire trip into the city with her face pressed to the window. Flynn spent most of the trip watching her. She gobbled up everything— the trees, the houses, the shops, the people.

She flinched as they passed a truck. 'It's so wrong driving on this side of the road.'

They drove on the left in Australia. In Germany it was the opposite. It took a bit of getting used to. As he watched her an ache he couldn't explain started up in his chest.

He rubbed a hand across it and forced his gaze away to stare out of his own window, but it didn't stop him from catching the tiny sounds she made— little gasps and tiny sighs that sounded like purrs. Each and every one of them pressed that ache deeper into him.

Maybe that was why, when the taxi deposited them at the front of their hotel, he snapped at her when she didn't follow after him at a trot, but stood glued to the footpath instead. He turned, rubbing a hand across his chest again. 'What are you doing?'

She glanced around as if memorising the buildings, the street and its layout. 'This is the very first time my feet have touched European ground.'

He opened his mouth to point out that technically that wasn't true.

'I want to fix it in my mind, relish the moment. I've dreamed of it for so long and I can hardly believe...'

He snapped his mouth shut again.

She suddenly stiffened, tossed him a glance, and before he knew what she was about she'd swung her hand luggage over her shoulder, seized both of their cases and was striding straight into the foyer of the hotel with them.

For pity's sake! He took off after her to find her enquiring, in perfect German no less, for a booking in the name of Mather.

The concierge smiled and welcomed her and double-checked the details of the booking.

Flynn moved up beside her. 'I didn't think you spoke German?' It came out like an accusation.

'I don't. I learned that phrase specifically.'

'For goodness' sake, why?'

'I thought it might come in handy, and to be polite, but...' She swallowed and turned back to the concierge and glanced at his name badge.

'*Entschuldigen Sie*—' I'm sorry '—Bruno, but I have no idea what you just said to me.'

The concierge beamed back at her. 'No matter at all, madam. Your accent was so perfect I thought you a native.'

'Now you're flattering me.' She laughed, delighted colour high on her cheeks. '*Danke.*' Thank you.

'*Bitte.*' You're welcome.

And from her smile Flynn could tell she knew what that meant. It was all he could do not to roll his eyes.

'Your hotel is sublime, beautiful.' She gestured around. 'And I can't tell you how excited I am to be here.'

The man beamed at her, completely charmed and this time Flynn did roll his eyes. 'And we're delighted to have you stay with us, madam.'

Given the prices they were charging, of course they were delighted.

Eventually Flynn managed to get their room keys and he pushed Addie in the direction of the elevator that silently whooshed them up four flights to the top floor.

Flynn stopped partway down the corridor. 'This should be your room.'

Her jaw dropped when she entered. 'It's huge!' She raced to the window. 'Oh, this is heaven.' She pointed. 'What's that?'

He moved to join her. 'That's called the Isartor. Munich was once a gated medieval city. Tor means gate. Isar is the name of the nearby river.'

She stared at him. 'So that's the gate to the river Isar. It sounds like something from a Grimm's fairy tale.'

She turned back to fully take in her room. 'Oh, Flynn, I don't need something this big.'

'I have the main suite next door and I wanted you nearby.'

She glanced around more slowly this time and her face fell. 'What?' he barked.

'I thought there might be an adjoining door.' Colour flared suddenly in her face. 'I mean, it's not that I want one. It's just they have them in the movies and…' She broke off, grimacing.

He had to laugh and it eased the burn in his chest. 'No adjoining doors, but feel free to come across and check out the suite.'

Flynn had never thought too much about hotel rooms before beyond space and comfort. And most of the time he didn't waste much thought on the second of those. Space mattered to him though. It probably had something to do with the wide open spaces of the cattle country he was used to. He didn't like feeling hemmed in. It was strange, then, that he spent so much of his time in the cities of Sydney and Brisbane.

'Oh, my! You have a walk-in closet. *And* a second bedroom!' Addie came hurtling back into the living area. 'You have all this—' she spread her arms wide to encompass the lounge area, dining table and kitchenette '—plus all that.' She pointed back the way she'd come from the bedrooms and bathroom.

The suite was generous.

She bounced on the sofa. She sat at the table. 'And it's all lovely light wood and blue and grey accents. It's beautiful.'

He glanced around. She was right. It was.

She poked about the minibar and straightened with a frown. 'There's no price list.'

'The minibar is included in the overall price. It's the same for your room.' When he travelled he wanted the best.

'No-o-o.' Her jaw dropped. 'You mean, I can drink and eat whatever I want from it and it won't cost you a penny more?'

Heck! Had he ever been that young? *Ja.*

'Fantastisch!'

She sobered. 'Thank you for my beautiful room.'

He rolled his shoulders. He hadn't been thinking of her comfort or enjoyment, but his own convenience. 'It's nothing. Don't think about it.'

'Thank you for bringing me to Munich.'

'It's not a free ride, Adelaide.'

'I know, and just you wait. I'm going to be the best PA you've ever had.'

Her sincerity pricked him. 'Addie, go and unpack your bags.'

Without so much as a murmur, she turned and left. Flynn collapsed onto the sofa, shaking his head. He eased back a bit further. Addie was right. The sofa was comfortable. He'd be able to rest here and—

Out of the blue it hit him then that not once between the airport and now had he given thought to the reason he was in Munich. He straightened. He pushed to his feet. Twenty years in the planning all ousted because of Addie's excitement? Jet lag. He grabbed his suitcase and strode into the master bedroom, started flinging clothes into the closet. Either that or he was going soft in the head.

He stowed the suitcase and raked both hands back through his hair. The important thing was that he was here now and that finally—after twenty years, twenty-two, to be precise—he had the means and opportunity to bring down the man who had destroyed his family. He would crush George Mueller the way George had laid waste to his father. And he intended to relish every moment of that with the same gusto Addie had so far shown for Munich.

With a grim smile, he made for the shower.

A knock sounded on the door and Flynn glanced up from his laptop. Housekeeping?

Or Addie?

He forced himself to his feet to open it. Addie stood on the other side, but it was a version of her he'd never seen before. What on earth? He blinked.

'May I come in?'

He moved aside to let her enter, his voice trapped somewhere between chest and throat. She sauntered in with a pot of coffee in one hand and a briefcase in the other. She wore a black business suit.

Hell's bells! Addie had legs that went on forever.

She set the briefcase on the table and the coffee pot on a trivet on the bench, before turning. He dragged his gaze from her legs. 'Where did you get that?' He pointed so she knew he meant the coffee, not the legs.

'The breakfast room.'

She collected two mugs and leant down to grab the milk from the bar fridge. Her skirt was a perfectly respectable length, but... He rubbed the nape of his neck. Who'd have known that beneath her jeans she'd have legs like that?

He shook himself. 'What are you doing?' The words practically bellowed from him. 'And why are you wearing that?'

Her face fell and he could've kicked himself. 'Sorry,' he ground out. 'Jet lag. That didn't come out right.'

She swallowed. 'Flynn, I know this trip isn't a free ride. So—' she gestured down at herself '—like a good *dainty* personal assistant, I donned my work clothes, made sure to get the boss coffee and now I'm here to put in a day's work.'

'I don't expect you to do any work today.'

She handed him a coffee. Strong and black. She must've remembered that from their meetings at Lorna Lee's. 'Why not?'

He took a sip. It wasn't as hot as he'd have liked, but he kept his trap shut on that head. She'd gone to the trouble of fetching it for him. Besides, it was excellent—brewed to perfection.

'I'm here to work,' she reminded him.

'Not on the day we fly in. You're allowed some time to settle in.'

'Oh.' She bit her lip. 'I didn't realise. You didn't say.'

'Where did you get the suit?' Had she bought it especially for the trip? He hadn't meant to put her out of pocket.

'I have a wardrobe full of suits. When I finished school I started an office administration course. I had plans to—'

She broke off and he realised that whatever plans she'd made, they hadn't come to fruition.

'But my mother became sick and I came home to help out and, well, the suits haven't really seen the light of day since.'

Because she'd been stuck on the farm. *Trapped* on the farm. He recalled the way she'd pressed her face against the window of the taxi, the look on her face as she'd stared around the city street below. Why was she in his room ready to work when she should be out there exploring the streets of Munich?

'Flynn, I don't even know what it is we're doing in Munich.'

That decided him. 'Go change into your warmer

clothes—jeans, a jumper and a coat—and I'll show you why we're here.'

Her eyes lit up. 'And a scarf, gloves and boots. I swear I've never known cold like this.'

'Wear two pairs of socks,' he called after her. 'I'll meet you in the foyer in ten minutes.'

Addie made it down to the foyer in eight minutes to find Flynn already there. She waved to Bruno, who waved back.

'Good to know you can move when necessary,' Flynn said, gesturing her towards the door.

Addie could hardly believe she was in Munich! She practically danced out of the door.

She halted outside. Which way did he want to go? Where did he mean to take her? Oh, goodness, it was cold! She tightened her scarf about her throat and stamped her feet up and down. 'It was thirty-three degrees Celsius when we left Sydney. The predicted top for Munich today is four!'

'In a couple of days you won't even notice.'

She turned to stare at him.

'Okay, you'll notice, but it won't hurt so much.'

'I'll accept that. So, what are you going to show me?'

'We're going to get our bearings first.'

Excellent plan. She pulled the complimentary map she'd found in her room from her coat pocket at the exact moment he pulled the same map from his.

He stared at her map, then at her and shook his head.

'What? I didn't want to get lost.' In rural Australia getting lost could get you killed.

'There's nothing dainty about you, is there, Addie?'

'Not if you're using dainty as a synonym for helpless,' she agreed warily. If it was important to him she supposed she could try and cultivate it, though.

He shoved his map back into his pocket. 'While we're on the subject, for the record I do not want you carrying my luggage.'

'Okay. Noted.' Man, who knew that negotiating the waters of PA and boss politics could be so tricky? 'Okay, while we're on the subject. When we're in business meetings and stuff, do you want me to call you Mr Mather and sir?'

His lip curled. 'Sir?'

Okay, she didn't need a business degree to work out his thoughts on that. 'So we're Herr Mather and his super-efficient—' and dainty if she could manage it '—PA, Addie.'

'Herr Mather and his assistant, Adelaide,' he corrected.

A little thrill shot up her spine. Adelaide sounded so grown up. It was a proper name for a PA. 'Right.'

Brrr…if they didn't move soon, though, she'd freeze to the footpath. She glanced at the map in her hand and then held it out to him. She could read a map as well as the next person, but she was well aware that the male of the species took particular pride in his navigational skills.

'You haven't been to Munich before?' she asked as he unfolded the map.

'No. What made you think I had?'

He studied the map and a lock of chestnut hair fell onto his forehead. The very tips were a couple of shades lighter and they, along with his tan, seemed at odds with all of this frosty cold. It made him seem suddenly exotic.

Deliciously exotic.

Delicious? She frowned. Well, she knew he was perfectly perfect—she'd known that the moment he'd stepped onto Lorna Lee's dressed in a perfectly perfect suit. He was also decidedly male. That had become evident the moment she'd clapped eyes on him in jeans and boots. She just hadn't felt all of that down in her gut until this very moment. She swallowed. Now she felt it all the way to her bones.

Flynn Mather was a perfect specimen of perfectly perfect maleness. In fact, if he'd been a stud bull she'd have moved heaven and earth to have him on the books at Lorna Lee's and—

'Addie?'

She snapped out of it. She swallowed. 'Sorry, brain fog, jet lag, the cold, I don't know.' What had they been talking about? She couldn't remember. She stared at the map and pointed. 'So where are we? What do I need to know?'

'Medieval walled city, remember?'

'Yep.' Nothing wrong with her memory.

'This circle here encloses the heart of the city. Most of our negotiations will take place within this area.'

She followed his finger as it went around, outlining where he meant. A tanned finger. A strong, tanned, masculine finger.

She had a feeling that perfectly perfect PAs didn't notice their boss's fingers.

'Our hotel is here.' His finger tapped the big blue star emblazoned with the hotel's name. 'Marienplatz—the town square—is the heart of it all and it's here...which is only a couple of blocks away.'

She jolted away from him in excitement. 'Oh, let's start there! I've read so much—'

She choked her words back. Perfectly perfect PAs waited to find out what was required of them. They didn't take the bit between their teeth and charge off.

'I mean only if it's convenient, of course, and part of your plan.'

He stared down at her and, while Munich was cold, the sky was blue but not as blue as Flynn's eyes. He grinned, and warmth—as if an oven door had been opened—encompassed her. 'You're trying really hard, aren't you?'

She couldn't deny it. 'Very.'

'I'd be happier if you'd just relax a bit.'

She bit her lip. 'I just want to do a good job and not let you down.'

'Wrong answer.'

She stared back at him. 'What was I supposed to say?'

'Noted,' he drawled and she couldn't help but laugh.

She could do relaxed…perfectly. 'To be honest, Flynn, I don't care which way we go, but can we move, please, before my feet freeze solid?'

He took her arm, his chuckle a frosty breath on the air. 'Right this way.'

He turned them towards Marienplatz. She stared at the shop fronts they passed, the people and the clothes they wore, the cars...but when she glanced up her feet slid to a halt.

'What now?' Flynn asked with exaggerated patience.

She pointed. 'Spires,' she whispered. *Oh, Robbie!* 'And green domes.'

'Pretty,' he agreed.

There was nothing like this in Australia. *Nothing.* A lump lodged in her throat. She'd never seen anything more beautiful.

'If you like those you should go to Paris. They have green domes enough to gladden every soul.'

No. She forced her legs forward again. She was *exactly* where she ought to be.

When they entered the town square, full of bustle and people on this bright chilly morning, and made their way to its centre even Flynn was quiet for a moment. 'That's really something,' he finally said.

All Addie could do was nod. Gothic architecture, sweeping spires, gargoyles and a glockenspiel were all arrayed in front of her. 'What more could one want from a town hall?' she breathed.

On cue, the glockenspiel rang out a series of notes. She and Flynn shared a glance and then folded their arms and stood shoulder to shoulder to watch. Addie had to keep closing her mouth as the jesters jested, the couples danced and the knights duelled. She watched as if in a dream, Flynn's shoulder solid against hers reminding her that this was all for real. She soaked it in, marvelled at it, her heart expanding with gratitude. The show lasted for fifteen minutes, and, despite the cold and the sore neck from craning upwards, she could've watched for another fifteen.

She spun to Flynn. 'Can you imagine how amazed the first people who ever saw that must've been? It would have been the height of technology at the time and—'

She suddenly realised she was holding his arm and, in her enthusiasm, was squeezing it. With a grimace and a belated pat of apology, she let it go. 'Sorry, got carried away.' It certainly wasn't dainty to pull your boss's arm out of its socket.

His lips twitched.

No, no—she didn't want to amuse him. She wanted to impress him.

She gestured back to the glockenspiel. 'And they call that the *New* Town Hall. I mean, it's gothic and—'

He turned her ninety degrees to face back the way they'd come. 'Oh!' A breath escaped her. 'And that would be the Old Town Hall and as it's medieval then I guess that makes sense.'

She turned a slow circle trying to take it all in.

'What do you think?'

He sounded interested in her impression. She wondered if he was merely humouring her. 'I can't believe how beautiful it all is.' She turned back to the New Town Hall and her stomach plummeted. An ache started up in her chest. 'Oh,' she murmured. 'I forgot.'

'Forgot what?'

'That it's Christmas.'

'Addie, there're decorations everywhere, not to mention a huge Christmas tree right there. How could you forget?'

She'd been too busy taking in the breathtaking architecture and the strangeness of it all. She lifted a shoulder. 'It's been such a rush this last week.' What with signing the contract to sell Lorna Lee's and preparing for the trip, Christmas had been the last thing on her mind.

Christmas. Her first ever Christmas away from Lorna Lee's. Her first Christmas without her father.

The ache stretched through her chest. If her father were still alive they'd have decorated their awful plastic tree—loaded it with tinsel and coloured balls and tiny aluminium bells and topped it with a gaudy angel. She'd be organising a ham and a turkey roll and—

A touch on her arm brought her back with a start. 'Where did you just go?'

His eyes were warm and soft and they eased the ache inside her. She remembered the way his eyes had blazed when she'd asked him if he knew what it was like to want something so terribly badly.

Yes, he'd known. She suspected he'd understand this too. 'The ghost of Christmases past,' she murmured. 'It's the first Christmas without my father.'

His face gentled. 'I'm sorry.'

'I've been doing my best not to think about it.' She stared across at the giant decorated tree that stood out at the front of the New Town Hall. 'I'm glad I'm spending Christmas here this year rather than on the farm.'

He nodded.

She turned back to him. 'Are your parents still alive?'

'My father isn't.'

Her lungs cramped at the desolation that momentarily stretched through his eyes. 'I'm sorry.'

He shoved his hands into the pockets of his coat. 'It was a long time ago.'

'Your mother?'

'My mother and I are estranged.'

She grimaced and shoved her hands into her pockets too. 'Oh, I'm sorry.' She shouldn't have pressed him.

He shrugged as if it didn't make an ounce of difference to him, but she didn't believe that for a moment. 'She's a difficult woman.'

She pushed her shoulders back. 'Then we'll just have to have our own orphans' Christmas in Munich.'

He opened his mouth. She waited but he closed it again. She cleared her throat, grimaced and scratched a hand through her hair. 'I, the thing is, I've just realised in the rush of it all that I haven't bought presents for the people back home.'

He stared down at her for three beats and then he laughed as if she'd shaken something loose from him. 'Addie, that's not going to be a problem. Haven't you heard about the Munich Christmas markets?'

'Markets?' She wanted to jump up and down. 'Really?'

'Some are held in this very square. You'll find presents for everyone.'

'There'll be time for that?' She could send the gifts express post to make sure they arrived on time. Hang the expense.

'Plenty of time.'

She folded her arms and surveyed him. 'When are you going to tell me what your business in Munich is?'

'Come right this way.' He took her arm and set off past the New Town Hall. They passed what looked like the main shopping area. She slanted a glance up at him. 'We'll still be in Munich for the post-Christmas sales, right?'

'Never stand in the way of a woman and the sales. Don't worry; you'll have time to shop.'

Cool.

She shook herself. That was all well and good, but when were they in fact going to do any work?

Eventually he stopped, let go of her arm and pointed. She peered at the building he gestured to. It took her a moment, but… 'Ooh, a beer hall! Can we…? I mean, is it too early…?'

'It's nearly midday. C'mon.' He ushered her inside.

The interior was enormous and filled with wooden tables and benches. He led her to a table by the wall, where they had a perfect view of the rest of the room. He studied the menu and ordered them both beers in perfect German.

She stared at her glass when it was set down in front of her—her very tall glass. 'Uh, Flynn, you ordered me half a litre of beer?'

'We could've ordered it by the litre if you'd prefer.'

Her jaw dropped as a barmaid walked past with three litre tankards in one hand and two in the other.

'Bottoms up!'

He sounded younger than she'd ever heard him. She raised her glass. 'Cheers.'

She took a sip and closed her eyes in bliss. 'Nectar from the gods. Now tell me what we're drinking to?'

'This—' he gestured around '—is what we're doing here.'

It took a moment. When she realised what he

meant she set her glass down and leaned towards him. 'You're buying the beer hall?' A grin threatened to split her face in two. That had to be every Australian boy's dream.

How perfectly perfect!

CHAPTER THREE

Dear Daisy

Munich is amazing. Gorgeous. And so cold! After a couple of hours out my face burned when I came back inside as if it were sunburned. Everything here is so different from Mudgee. I know it's not Paris, but it's marvellous just the same.

You know, it got me thinking about starting the blog back up, but...I'd simply be searching for something I can't have. Again.

You should be here in Europe with me. You should... Sorry, enough of that. Guess what? I finally found out what we're doing here. The perfectly perfect F is buying a brewery that has its own beer hall! How exciting is that?

We have our very first business meeting at eleven o'clock this morning. I'm going to wear that gorgeous garnet-coloured suit I bought in Sydney when we went to see Cate Blanchett at the theatre that time. I have no idea what I'm

*supposed to do in said meeting, but in that suit
I'll at least look the part!
Wish you were here.
Love, Buttercup*

ADDIE EXITED HER *Till the Cows Come Home* Word document, closed the lid of her laptop and resisted the urge to snuggle back beneath the covers. It was only seven a.m. She could sneak in another hour of shut-eye. Flynn had said he didn't need to see her until quarter to eleven in his room, where the meeting was scheduled to take place, but...

She was in Munich!

She leapt out of bed, smothering a yawn. A brisk walk down by the River Isar would be just the thing. She wanted her body clock on Munich time asap. What she didn't want was any more of the crazy disturbed sleep like that she'd had last night.

A walk *in Munich* would wake her up, enliven her and have her bright-eyed and bushy-tailed for Flynn's business meeting.

Perfect.

Addie tried to stifle a yawn as the lawyer droned on and on and on about the conditions of probate and the details of the contract negotiations that were under way, plus additional clauses that would need to be considered, along with local government regulations and demands and…on and on and on.

Did Flynn find this stuff interesting?

She glanced at him from the corner of her eye. He watched the lawyer narrowly, those blue eyes alert. She sensed the tension coiled up inside him as if he were a stroppy King Brown waiting to strike, even as he leaned back in his seat, the picture of studied ease. She wondered if the lawyer knew.

She shivered, but she couldn't deny it only made him seem more powerful…and lethal, like a hero from a thriller. It must be beyond brilliant to feel that confident, to have all of that uncompromising derring-do. One could save small children from burning buildings and dive into seething seas to rescue battered shipwreck victims and—

'Make a note of that, will you, please, Adelaide?'

She crashed back into the room, swallowing. She pulled her notebook towards her without glancing at Flynn and jotted on it.

Am making notes about nothing so as to look efficient. Listen in future, Addie! Pay attention.

She underlined 'listen' three times.

Biting back a sigh, she tried to force her attention back to the conversation—the negotiations—but the lawyer was droning on and on in that barely varying monotone. If he'd been speaking German she'd have had a reason for tuning out, but he was speaking English with an American accent and it should've had her riveted, but...

For heaven's sake, the subject matter was so dry and dull that he could've had the most gorgeous and compelling voice in the world and she'd still tune out. She mentally scrubbed property developer off her list of potential future jobs. And lawyer.

She glanced at Flynn again. He wore a charcoal business suit and looked perfect. Didn't he feel the slightest effect from jet lag? Perhaps he really was a machine?

She bit back another sigh. Perhaps he was just a seasoned world traveller who was used to brokering million-dollar deals.

The figures these two were bandying about had almost made her eyes pop. She'd wanted to tug on Flynn's sleeve and double-check that he really wanted to invest that much money in a German brewery.

Sure, he was an Aussie guy. Aussie guys—

and girls, for that matter—and beer went hand in hand. But there were limits, surely? Even for high-flying Flynn.

Still, she knew what it was like to have a childhood dream. Good luck to him for making his a reality.

She had a sudden vision of him galloping across the fields at Lorna Lee's on Blossom. She leaned back. Did he really prefer this kind of wheeling and dealing to—?

'Record that number, please, Adelaide.'

She started and glanced at the lawyer, who barked a series of numbers at her. She scribbled them down. Was it a phone number or a fax number? For all she knew it was a serial number for… She drew a blank. She scrawled a question mark beside it.

In her pocket her phone vibrated. She silently thanked the patron saint of personal assistants for giving her the insight to switch it to silent. She slid it out and her lips lifted. A message from Frank. She clicked on it, eager for news from home.

This man of Flynn's wants to get rid of Bruce Augustus.

Her hand clenched about the phone. She shot to her feet. 'Over my dead body!'

The lawyer broke off. Both he and Flynn stared at her. She scowled at Flynn. 'This foreman of yours and I are going to have serious words.'

He cocked an eyebrow.

She recalled where they were and what they were supposed to be doing and cleared her throat, took her seat again. 'Later,' she murmured. 'We'll have our serious words later.'

But she messaged back to Frank.

If he does he dies. Text me his number.

Flynn stretched out a long leg, leaning further back in his chair, reminding her even more vividly of a King Brown. Addie pocketed her phone and kept a close eye on him.

'So what you're in effect telling me, Herr Gunther, is that there's going to be a delay in probate.'

When Flynn spoke she had no trouble whatsoever paying attention. The lawyer hummed and hawed and tried to squeeze his way out of the corner Flynn had herded him into, but there was no evading Flynn. She wondered if he'd ever camp drafted. She'd bet he'd be good at it. With those shoulders...

She blinked and shifted on her seat. She didn't care about shoulders. What she cared about was Bruce Augustus.

And getting off the farm.

She rolled her eyes. Yeah, right, as if she'd scaled the heights of PA proficiency today. She'd need to do better if she wanted this job for real.

You have a month.

'Are you familiar with the law firm Schubert, Schuller and Schmidt?'

The lawyer nodded.

'I've hired them to represent me. You'll be hearing from them.'

'I—'

Flynn rose and the lawyer's words bumbled to a halt. Addie stood too and fixed the lawyer with what she hoped was a smile as pleasantly cool as Flynn's. Thank goodness this was over.

'Thank you for your time, Herr Gunther. It was most instructive.'

Was it? Addie ushered the lawyer towards the door with an inane, 'Have a nice day, Herr Gunther,' all the while impatience building inside her.

The door had barely closed before she pulled her

cell phone from her pocket and punched in Howard's number.

'What's he done?' Flynn asked as she strode back towards the table.

'Nothing you need to worry about. I'll deal with it.'

He opened his mouth and it suddenly occurred to her what nicely shaped lips he had. It wasn't something she generally noticed about a man, but Flynn definitely—

'Hello?'

She snapped to attention. 'Howard, it's Adelaide Ramsey.'

He swore. 'Do you know what time it is in Australia?'

'I don't care what time it is.' That only made it worse. It meant Frank and Jeannie had been fretting till all hours. 'Now listen to me very carefully. If you harm one hair on Bruce Augustus's head, if you try to send him to the knackers, I will have your guts for garters. Do you hear me?'

'But—'

'No buts!'

'Look, Addie, I understand—'

'Have you ever owned a farm, Howard?' She shifted, suddenly aware of how closely Flynn watched her. She swallowed and avoided eye contact.

'No.'

'Then you don't understand.'

A pause followed. 'The boss has given me the authority to make changes, Addie, and Bruce Augustus is dead wood.'

Dead wood! She could feel herself start to shake.

'I have the boss's ear and—'

She snorted. 'You have his ear? Honey, I have more than his ear. I'm going to *be* your boss when I return home—you realise that, don't you? You do *not* want to get on the wrong side of me.'

Silence sounded and this time Howard didn't break it. 'Goodnight, Howard.' With that she snapped her phone shut and swung to face Flynn.

His lips twitched. 'Sorted, huh?'

Was he laughing at her? She narrowed her gaze and pocketed her phone. 'Absolutely.'

He lowered himself to the sofa. 'Can you tell me exactly why Bruce Augustus is necessary to Lorna Lee's future?'

'Because if he goes—' she folded her arms '—I go.'

He leaned forward and she found herself on the

receiving end of a gaze colder than a Munich winter. 'We have a deal. You signed a contract.'

She widened her stance. 'You mess with my bull and the deal's off. There's a six-week cooling-off period to that contract, remember? You threaten my bull and I'll pull out of the sale.'

He leaned back. She couldn't read his expression at all. 'You mean that,' he eventually said.

She tried to stop her shoulders from sagging and nodded. She meant it.

'Why is he so important to you?'

She would never be able to explain to him what a friend the bull had been to her. It was pointless even to try. 'You said one of the reasons you wanted me to remain at Lorna Lee's was due to the affinity I have with the animals.'

'I believe the term I used was stock.'

'You can use whatever term you like—you can try and distance yourself from them—but it doesn't change what they are.'

'Which is?'

'Living creatures that provide us with our livelihoods. We have a culture at Lorna Lee's of looking after our own. I consider it a duty. *That's* where my so-called affinity comes from. When an animal provides us with good service we don't repay that by getting rid of them when they're past their use-by date. They get to live out their days in easy retirement. If that's a culture you can't live with, Flynn, then you'd better tell me now.'

He pursed his lips and continued to survey her. It took all of her strength not to fidget. 'I can live with it,' he finally said. 'Do you want it in writing?'

Very slowly she let out a breath. 'No. I believe you're a man of your word.'

He blinked. She held out her hand and he rose and shook it.

For no reason at all her heart knocked against her ribs. She pulled her hand free again, but her heart didn't stop pounding.

'Howard?' Flynn held his cell phone to his ear.

'Yes, I do. Just…don't touch the bull.'

He listened then. Obviously to the other man's justifications. She scowled. There were no justifications for—

'Howard wants to know if you're okay with him dredging the dam in the western paddock of the Seymour place…'

Oh, yes, that was long overdue.

'…extending the irrigation system on the southern boundary…'

There'd be money for that?

'...and installing solar panels on the roofs of all the homesteads?'

She swallowed and nodded. 'Those things all sound great. I don't have a problem with improvements.'

Flynn spoke to Howard for a few moments more and then rang off.

She swung back to him. 'When I return to the farm, who's going to be in charge—him or me?'

'I'll be in charge, Addie.'

Oops, that was right. Still, if rumour were anything to go by, Flynn didn't stay in any one spot for too long.

'You and Howard will have authority over different areas. You'll be in charge of the breeding programme. He'll be in charge of overseeing major improvements. I'll be overseeing the two of you.'

Unless she managed to change his mind by turning into the perfect PA. Which reminded her...

'I'm sorry I had that outburst in the meeting.'

He shrugged. 'It needed something to liven it up.'

It didn't change the fact that she should've had more presence of mind than to shout out during a business meeting. She bit her lip and glanced at him. 'So, you didn't find that meeting riveting?'

'Absolutely not.'

She sagged. 'I thought it might've just been me. Jet lag or something.' She retrieved her notebook and handed it to him. 'I'm really sorry, but my mind kept drifting off.'

He laughed when he read her notes—or lack of them.

'I promise to do better next time.'

He handed the notebook back. 'I only asked you to jot things down to keep myself awake.'

She wrinkled her nose. 'Are all business meetings that dull?'

'Not at all. Herr Gunther was just doing his best to bore and obfuscate.'

He'd succeeded with her. 'Why?'

'Because he favours one of my rivals and is hoping this other party can get a jump on me somehow.'

'There's a rival?'

'There're several, but only the one we need worry about.'

'Will this rival get a jump on you? Should we be worried?'

His eyes suddenly blazed and one of his hands clenched. 'I say bring it on. The harder and the dirtier the battle, the more satisfying it'll be.'

Really?

'Regardless of the cost, Addie, this is one battle I mean to win.'

She swallowed. Right.

'The upshot of the meeting is that there's been a delay in processing probate.'

The one thing Addie had fathomed from the meeting was that the person who'd owned the premises that housed the brewery and beer hall had recently died. Hence the reason the property would soon be on the market. The probate referred to the reading of this man's will so his estate could be finalised.

'Herr Gunther will try to draw that delay out for as long as he can, but we're not going to let him.'

That made them sound thrillingly powerful and masterful. She clapped her hands. 'So?'

He raised an eyebrow. 'So?'

'What next? Do we head over to these Schubert, Schuller and Schmidt's of yours and come up with a game plan?'

'They already have my instructions. You, Adelaide Ramsey, have the rest of the day off to do whatever you want.'

Really? That was the entirety of her work for the day?

'Go out and explore. Sightsee.' He glanced up

when she didn't move. 'If I need you I have your mobile number. I'll call you if something comes up.'

Right. She gathered up her things.

'And, Addie?'

She turned in the doorway. 'Yes?'

'Have fun.'

Oh, she meant to, but she wouldn't be sightseeing in this gorgeous and compelling city. At least, not this afternoon. If she wanted to convince Flynn that she was perfect PA material, she had work to do.

Flynn barely glanced up from his laptop when the room phone rang. He seized it and pressed it to his ear. 'Hello?'

'Flynn, it's Addie. I wondered if you were busy.'

He closed the lid of his laptop, her threat to pull out of the sale still ringing in his ears. He wondered if she realised how fully invested in Lorna Lee's she was. And if he hadn't been aware of his own emotional stake in the place before, he was now. 'Not busy at all. What's up?'

'Would it be convenient to come over to show you something I've been working on?'

She'd been working? On what? 'The door's open.'

He replaced the receiver with a smothered curse

and unlocked the door—stood there holding it wide open, like a lackey. Darn it! She wasn't going to pull out of their deal, was she? Lorna Lee's was small fry in the grand scheme of things, but…he'd started to think of it as a place he could hang his hat. He didn't have one of those. It was disconcerting to discover that he wanted one, but he refused to bury the need. Lorna Lee's would be perfect.

Addie came tripping in with her laptop under one arm and her notepad clutched to her chest. She'd swapped her saucy red suit for jeans and a long-sleeved T-shirt. She moved straight to the table and fired the laptop to life without a word, but a smile lit her lips and a pretty colour bloomed high on her cheeks. When she turned those amber eyes to him, their brightness made his heart sink.

If she loved her home that much he'd never be able to take it away from her.

Would she consider going into a partnership with him instead?

'I've spent the afternoon researching breweries and beer halls and—'

'You've what?' The door slipped from his fingers and closed with a muted whoosh. 'For heaven's sake, why?'

Her hands went to her hips. 'You're buying one, aren't you?'

'Specifically, I'm buying the premises.'

She waved a hand in the air. 'Semantics.'

He decided not to correct her.

'Bavaria is known for its fine beer. And, of course, Munich is famous for Oktoberfest.'

He rubbed his nape. 'Addie, why aren't you out there seeing the sights and experiencing the delights of Munich?'

She clicked away on her computer. 'I want to be useful.'

He closed his eyes and counted to three. 'What happened to "have you ever wanted something so bad", et cetera? This is a once-in–a-lifetime opportunity.'

She spun to stare at him. 'And buying a brewery and beer hall isn't?'

His mouth opened and closed, but no sound came out. He shook himself. 'C'mon.' He took her arm and propelled her out of the room, grabbing his coat and scarf on the way. 'Go put on a jumper and scarf and coat.'

'But don't you want to hear about the research I did and—?'

'Later.'

He waited outside her door while she grabbed her things.

'If you really want to be useful to me, Addie, then I want you out and about in Munich seeing and experiencing everything you can.'

She stared at him as they made their way down the stairs, struggling to get her arms into her coat. 'You want me to immerse myself in the culture?' She bit her lip. 'Are you hoping that whatever insights I gain might be helpful in your negotiations somehow?'

If she thought that was the reason then he'd play along. He held her coat so she could get her left arm in the sleeve. 'Yes.'

'Oh.' She glared at him. 'Then why didn't you say so?'

Because he hadn't been fool enough to think she'd waste the best part of a day researching breweries when it wasn't even breweries he was interested in.

Not that she knew that.

'Really, Flynn,' she harrumphed. 'You need to give your people better information.'

'Noted,' he said and had the pleasure of seeing her lips twitch. He wanted her to sightsee until she was sick of it. He wanted her to get the wanderlust out of her system so she'd settle back at Lorna Lee's without chafing at imaginary restraints.

They're not imaginary.

Whatever! She'd get four weeks' annual leave a year and plane tickets wherever she wanted. He didn't want her getting the wanderlust so completely out of her system that she refused to sell her farm to him.

She belted the sash of her coat all the more securely about her when they stepped outside. 'It gets dark so quickly here. It's barely five o'clock.'

He missed Australia's warmth and daylight savings. Back home night wouldn't fall for another four hours. 'That's the joys of a northern hemisphere winter,' was all he said.

'Where are we going?'

He'd considered that while waiting outside her door. 'You said you needed to buy Christmas presents, and I expect you'd like to mail them home in time for Christmas.'

Her face lit up. 'The Christmas markets?'

Better yet. 'The *medieval* Christmas markets.'

Her eyes widened. 'Oh.' She clasped her gloved hands beneath her chin. 'That sounds perfectly perfect.'

He glanced down at her and something shifted

in his chest. Silly woman! Why had she wasted her precious time cooped up inside? She didn't strike him as the type who'd be afraid to venture forth on her own.

I want to be useful.

He bit back a sigh. Yeah, well, he didn't want her crying on her own in Bruce Augustus's pen in the future. 'Just so you know,' he said, turning them in the direction of Wittelsbacherplatz—the site of the markets, 'this isn't some touristy money spinner.' Though no doubt it did that too. 'There's been a Christmas market on the site since medieval times apparently.'

Her jaw dropped when a short while later they passed one of the façades of the Residenz—a series of palaces and courtyards that had been the home of former Bavarian rulers. 'That's… It's amazing.'

He stared too. It was really something.

They turned down the next boulevard and her eyes widened as if to take in all the beauty. He totally sympathised. When they stepped into Odeonsplatz and she clapped eyes on St Peter's Church, she came to a dead halt. She glanced around, blinking at the Field Marshal's Hall. 'How can one city have so much beauty?' she breathed.

'What do you think?'

'Words can't do it justice. It's beautiful. I love it.'

He grinned then. 'Come right this way.'

Less than a minute later they entered Wittelsbacherplatz. It was purported to be one of the most commanding squares in Munich and at the moment it was alive with colour and bustle and the scent of Christmas. Not to mention row upon row of market stalls.

He glanced down at her and his grin widened. Breweries and Lorna Lee's were the furthest things from her mind and he pushed them firmly from his too. 'C'mon. Let's start down here.' He took her arm and led her down one of the alleys formed by the stalls.

They lost themselves in a whole new world. There were woodcarvers, glass-blowers and bakers. There were shoemakers, cuckoo clocks and gingerbread. There was noise and life and vigour, and he watched as it brought Addie alive and filled her with delight. They stopped to watch a medieval dance troop perform a folk dance, the scents from the nearby food stalls filling the air. When the dance was complete she took his arm and headed down a different alley. 'This is amazing! Have you ever seen anything so amazing? It's just...'

His mouth hooked up. 'Amazing?'

'Nutcrackers!'

He glanced from her face to the items she pointed to. An entire stall was devoted to small, and not so small, wooden soldiers.

'Colin would love these!' She selected four and paid for them all on her own, never once asking him to interpret for her. He shook his head. She definitely wasn't afraid of venturing forth on her own.

I want to be useful.

He had overcome that barrier now, hadn't he?

She oohed and aahed over chimney sweeps made from dried plums and almonds. She bought some gingerbread.

'Uh, Addie, I'm not sure you'll get that through Australian customs.'

'Who said anything about posting this home? It's for us now.' She opened the bag and broke off a piece. He thought she might melt on the spot when she tasted it. She held the bag out to him and lunch suddenly seemed like hours ago. He helped himself to a slice. She grinned at whatever expression passed across his face. 'Good, isn't it?'

He took some more. 'Really good.'

He bought them mugs of *glühwein* and they drank it, standing around one of the makeshift fires that dotted the square, Addie's holiday mood infecting him. He drank in the Christmas goodness and watched as she tried to choose a wooden figurine for Frank. 'What do you think?' She turned, holding up two carvings for his inspection. 'Father Time or the billy goat?'

He could tell by the way she surveyed the goat that it was her favourite. He didn't doubt for a moment that Frank would love either of them. 'The goat.'

He took her parcels from her so she could browse unencumbered. They stopped to watch a glassblower shape a perfect snowflake—an ornament for a Christmas tree—but he preferred to watch her.

When was the last time he'd relished something as much as Addie was relishing this outing?

He frowned and tried to wipe the thought away. He didn't want to put any kind of dampener on Addie's mood. Not when she'd put in a full day's work on his behalf. He frowned again. He still didn't feel as if he'd got to the bottom of that yet.

'Oh, Flynn, look at that.'

He dutifully glanced at what she held out to him. It was an exquisite glass angel—ludicrously delicate and unbelievably detailed.

'Jeannie would go into ecstasies over this, but...'

'But?'

'It'd be in a thousand pieces before it ever reached her.'

He eyed it and then the packaging it came in. 'Not necessarily. It'd be well protected in its box with all of that tissue paper and sawdust around it. If we put it in another box with bubble wrap—' lots of bubble wrap '—and marked it fragile it should be fine.'

'You really think so?'

'The packaging and postage won't come cheap,' he warned.

'Hang the expense.' She bought it. It made her eyes bright. His shoulders swung suddenly free.

'Now who do you need to buy for?'

He blinked. Him? Nobody. 'I give bonuses, Addie, not Christmas gifts.'

'But surely you have friends who...' She trailed off.

Friends he hadn't spent enough time with over the last few years, he suddenly realised.

'I'm sorry. I didn't mean to make you sad.'

He shook himself. 'Not sad,' he countered. 'Wine. I've sent them wine. It's already been ordered.' One of his secretaries would've taken care of it.

She folded her arms. 'Surely there's a significant other out there you ought to buy some frippery for?'

He tried to look forbidding. 'I beg your pardon?'

She reddened. 'I'm not trying to pry.' She stiffened. 'And I don't want you thinking I'm putting myself forward for the position, mind, if there is a vacancy.'

Perhaps he'd overdone it on the forbidding thing. 'I'm not getting those vibes from you, Addie. If I were I'd make sure you were aware that I *never* get involved with employees.'

'Right.' She eased back a bit further to stare at him.

He rolled his shoulders. 'What?'

'Don't get me wrong, but you're young, successful and presentable.' She raised an eyebrow. 'Heterosexual?'

'As two failed marriages will attest.'

She shook her head. 'That doesn't prove—' Her jaw dropped. *Two failed marriages! Two?*

'Which is why I make sure *no* woman ever expects a Christmas present from me. I'm not travelling that particular road to hell ever again.'

'Two—' She gulped back whatever she'd been going to say and shook herself upright, gave one emphatic nod. 'Fair enough. The short answer is there's really nobody you need to buy for.'

'Correct.'

'The long answer is there's not going to be a new mistress at Lorna Lee's.'

Had she been worried about that? It made sense, he guessed. In her place he'd have wondered the same. 'Who else do you need to buy for?'

'Eric and Lucy.'

She'd bought a present for their little boy. Wasn't that enough?

'To own the truth, Flynn, I'm starting to feel a little shopped out.'

No, she wasn't. She'd only said that because she thought he must be bored with the shopping. He opened his mouth to disabuse her of the notion.

'What I am is starved.'

He glanced at his watch and did a double take. Seven o'clock? How had that happened? 'C'mon, we passed a cute-looking traditional place on the way here.'

The cute place turned out to be a beer hall. Of course. But Addie didn't seem to mind. 'I'll have the pork knuckle with the potato dumpling,' she said to the waitress, pointing to the dish on the menu.

Flynn held up two fingers. *'Zwei, bitte.'* He ordered two wheat beers as well.

'My research today informs me that one can't get more Bavarian than pork knuckle and dumpling.'

'Unless you settle for a plate of bratwurst,' he pointed out.

'I'll try that tomorrow.'

She stared at him. Eventually he raised his hands. 'What?'

'Aren't you even the slightest bit interested in all the stuff I've researched today?'

Not really. He didn't say that, though.

'For example, do you know how expensive beef is here?'

'Compared to Australian prices, beef is expensive throughout all of Europe.'

'You could make an absolute killing by supplying beef dishes at your beer hall. Beef sourced from your cattle station.'

He leaned towards her. She smelled of gingerbread and oranges. 'Why is doing a good job for me so important to you?'

'Oh.' She bit her lip and her gaze slid away. 'I, um…I was thinking that if I did a really good job for you, that you wouldn't mind providing me with a reference. A glowing reference I'll be able to use when I come back to Europe for real.'

'Addie, you are in Europe for real.'

She shook her head, her gaze returning to his. 'This is time out of time, not real life.'

What on earth was she talking about?

'When my two years are up on Lorna Lee's I'll be leaving to lead my real life.'

Her real life?

'And my real life is working my way through Europe at my leisure.'

Why was she so determined to leave a place that had nurtured her, a place she obviously loved, for a hobo temping trek around Europe? For heaven's sake, she'd be bored to death as a PA. Wasn't to-day's meeting proof positive of that?

'Unless of course you find that I'm the best PA you've ever had and decide you can't be doing without me.'

He laughed.

Addie glanced down at the table.

The waitress arrived with their beers and he lifted his glass in salute. 'To enjoying Munich.'

When she lifted her gaze he could've sworn her eyes swam, but she saluted him with her glass, blinding him with a big bright smile. 'To Munich.'

CHAPTER FOUR

FLYNN CLOSED THE door to his room and flung his coat and scarf on a chair. Pushing his hands into the small of his back, he stretched. His body ached, which didn't make a whole lot of sense. All he'd done was walk and talk, eat and laugh. It wasn't as if he'd been on muster.

He glanced at his watch and blew out a breath. Eleven p.m. He'd been walking and talking and eating and laughing for six hours. He moved to the window to stare down at the now quiet street below. He hadn't expected to enjoy Munich. He'd come here to get a job done. Enjoyment hadn't been on the agenda. Somewhere along the way, though, Addie's delight in the Christmas markets had proved contagious.

From his pocket he pulled the carved wooden bull he'd bought when Addie hadn't been looking. He'd meant to give it to her during dinner as a gesture of goodwill, a promise that Bruce Augustus would always have a home at Lorna Lee's, but, while there was no denying that Addie was good company, there'd been a shift in...tone, mood, temper? He hadn't been able to put his finger on it, but Addie had somehow subtly distanced herself and the carved bull had remained in his pocket—the right moment never presenting itself.

He frowned. It'd been a long time since he'd shared a convivial meal with a friend. Not that Addie was a friend—she was an employee—but it had him thinking about his real friends. Wasn't it time to enjoy the fruits of his labours and slow down on the cut-and-thrust? It wasn't a question he'd ever considered. Now he couldn't get it out of his mind.

He swung away from the window. What? A slip of a girl milked every ounce of enjoyment from a new experience and now he was questioning his entire way of life?

He shook himself. There was nothing wrong with being goal-oriented!

He rubbed his nape. But, when *was* the last time he'd enjoyed something as wholeheartedly as Addie?

He collapsed to the sofa. Maybe it was time to slow down. After he'd brought ruin down on Mueller's head, of course.

He recalled the peace that had filtered through his soul when he'd first clapped eyes on the rolling fields of Lorna Lee's. When he left Munich maybe he could focus on spending time there, working the land and building a home. The idea eased the ball of tightness in his chest.

First, though, he had to deal with Mueller. That fist clenched up tight again. With a growl, he headed for the shower.

It wasn't until he emerged, rubbing a towel over his hair, that Flynn noticed Addie's laptop and note-pad sitting on the dining table. He paused, hesitated and then flipped open the notepad. Nothing. She'd obviously brought it along to make notes.

He eyed the laptop, rolled his shoulders and stretched his neck, first to the right and then to the left. He didn't care about the brewery. He only cared about ruining Mueller.

Still, he'd have to do something with the premises. The local council wouldn't allow them to remain idle. He'd need to provide them with assurances, make promises. Besides, it wouldn't hurt to look at the material Addie had gathered *in her free time*.

He seized the computer, planted himself on the sofa and fired it up. He'd be careful not to look at any personal documents. Clicking on the last word-processing document she'd been working one—the one titled Flynn's Brewery/Beer Hall—he read her rough notes.

He straightened. Actually, while some of her ideas were fairly basic, some of them were interesting and surprisingly savvy.

He opened her Internet browser to follow a couple of references she'd made in her notes. He pursed his lips, his mind starting to race. Once he'd bought the premises out from beneath Mueller, it wouldn't be too hard to establish another brewery there—the equipment belonged to the premises, which meant it'd meet local council regulations.

He grinned and lifted a foot to the coffee table. Mueller's finances were in a sorry state. He'd invested too heavily in improvements to the premises without securing a guarantee—*in writing*—that he'd have first option to buy if they ever came on the market. A gentleman's agreement didn't count in this situation. A harsh laugh broke from him. That was just as well. Mueller was no gentleman. He might be able to make a halfway decent offer on the premises, but Flynn would be able to offer three times as much.

He rested his head back and stared up at the ceiling, satisfaction coursing through him. Running a brewery on Mueller's premises? Talk about poetic justice. Talk about rubbing salt into the wound.

He glanced at the computer again. The idea of owning a brewery hadn't filled him with any enthusiasm except as a means to an end. It could just as well have been a sausage factory for all he cared. But now...

Addie's enthusiasm, he discovered, wasn't just reserved for her travels—it filled her notes too and some of it caught fire in his veins. Owning a beer hall could be fun. Hadn't he just decided he needed more fun in his life? He settled back and checked her word-processing file history and then selected a document titled 'Till the Cows Come Home.' He figured it'd have something to do with the beef industry. Her idea of using beef supplied from his cattle station to launch a cheaper beef menu had a lot of merit.

A document with a header of daisies and buttercups and cartoon cows appeared. He frowned. This looked personal. He went to close it when several words leapt out at him—Munich, Brewery and F.

Dear Daisy,
I know I've said it before, but I have to say it again—you'd love Munich as much as I do! I

know it's not Paris, but beggars can't be choosers—isn't that what they say? Anyway, you'd have a ball, turning all the guys' heads in one of the traditional Bavarian costumes the barmaids wear—very sexy.

We'd have to build up our arm muscles, though, before embarking on a barmaid career here. You wouldn't believe it, but I saw one girl carrying ten litres of beer—five litres in each hand—and she didn't even break a sweat. Amazing! I love the beer halls.

Hmm...wonder if F would leave me here as a tavern wench?

He grinned. Not a chance.

Speaking of which, the perfectly perfect F is perfectly cool and collected in business meetings too. Extraordinary that someone actually enjoys those things.

Still...I wish...with all my heart I wish you were here.
Love Buttercup.

Buttercup, huh?
So who was Daisy?

PS I've decided against starting the blog up again and—

Flynn jerked upright and hit 'quit' in double-quick time. He wasn't going to read Addie's private diary! Sheesh!

He stared at her computer screen, went to close down the internet browser when, on impulse, he typed 'Till the Cows Come Home' into the search engine. A page with a background of daisies, buttercups and cartoon cows loaded. He checked the archives. The very first post was dated six years ago. He read it. He read the next one and the one after that, battling the lump growing in his throat. He read into the wee small hours until he could no longer battle fatigue. In the morning when he woke he picked up where he'd left off.

Addie had posted every day for eighteen months, but the blog had been defunct for the last four years. He stared at the wall opposite. Was it an invasion to read her blog like this? If she'd truly wanted privacy she'd have kept a diary instead, right? As she did now. He scrubbed a hand down his face before shutting off the computer and pulling on a pair of sweats.

She'd published it in a public forum. After all, that was what a blog was—a way of reaching out and connecting with other people. Only…comments had been left but Addie hadn't responded to any of them.

Who was Daisy? Addie had bared her soul in that blog—her pain and heartbreak when her friend—Daisy—had died of leukaemia.

He could ask her.

Or you could keep your fat trap shut.

None of it was his business.

So why did it feel as if it were?

He jerked around at the tap on his door. A quiet tap as if the person on the other side was being careful to not disturb him if he were still asleep. Instinct told him it'd be Addie. Asleep? Ha!

He pulled in a breath, careful to keep his face smooth, before opening the door. Addie had started to turn away, but she swung back and her smile hit him in the gut. 'Hey, good morning.'

'Morning.'

She eyed him carefully. 'You okay?'

He cleared his throat. 'Yep. Fine. All's good with me.'

She blinked and her brow furrowed and then she shook it all away. 'Sorry to disturb you, but I wondered if I could grab my laptop. I left it here yesterday. I forgot to collect it when we got back last night. Speaking of which, I laid down for just a moment and bang! I was out for the count. Jet lag's a killer, huh?'

He strove for casual, for normal, when all he really wanted to do was haul her in his arms and hug her tight, tell her how sorry he was about Daisy. He cleared his throat. 'Jet lag? But you stayed awake all day yesterday, right?'

She snorted. 'One could hardly call whatever I was in that meeting with the lawyer awake.'

He laughed, when he'd thought laughing would be beyond him.

'Fingers crossed, though, that the body clock is on local time now.'

He suddenly realised they both still stood by the door. He strode back into the room, seized her laptop and notepad and then swung back and thrust them at her. He didn't invite her inside. He hoped a bit of distance would help him get his thoughts and impulses under control and ease the burning in his chest when he glanced at her.

Everything he'd read, it was none of his business. That, however, didn't mean he could just push it out of his head, disregard it or forget it. It was still too close.

She clasped the computer and notepad to her chest. 'Is today still a free day?'

He nodded. Tomorrow he'd have a meeting with his lawyers, but it was only for form's sake—to keep him abreast of what they were doing and where they were at. They'd been quietly beavering away on his behalf for the last few weeks.

'Okay, well, while I have a chance to ask, what would you like me to prepare for tomorrow?'

'Nothing.' In fact, she wouldn't even need to attend.

'You haven't given me so much as a letter to type up yet!'

But she wanted to help, to be useful. He leaned against the door. 'You want the truth?'

She stuck out a hip and nodded.

'Many of these kinds of negotiations are about appearances.'

She stared at him as if waiting for more. 'Okay.' She drew the word out.

'While we're here I want—need—to appear powerful, in control and ruthless.'

She lifted a shoulder. 'As you're all those things then I don't see the problem.'

She thought him ruthless?

He rubbed his nape. Of course she did. He was

all but forcing her to spend the next two years at Lorna Lee's. 'I know I am and you know I am...'

'Ah, but you need the people you're negotiating with to know that you are too.'

'And the sooner, the better. How do you think I can best achieve that?'

'By dressing smartly in expensive suits and staying in swish hotels?'

'And having lackeys.'

Her face cleared. 'I'm your lackey!'

'Not literally, you realise.'

'But *they* don't know that.' She chewed her lip. 'So I just have to dress smartly, say "Yes, Mr Mather" and "No, Mr Mather" at the appropriate times, fetch you coffee when you demand it, email London when you tell me to, and ring New York when you deem it necessary.'

'Now you're getting the hang of it.'

She beamed at him. 'I could do that with my eyes closed.'

He frowned.

'Except I won't, of course.'

'I have perfect faith in your abilities, Adelaide.'

She stared at him for a moment before shaking herself. 'So you don't have plans for this afternoon and this evening?'

'I...'

'Because I'm going to try and get us tickets to the ice hockey.'

He stared at her.

'Sport is a universal language, Flynn.'

In her diary she'd called him perfectly perfect and it hadn't sounded like a compliment.

'So you never know. A passing comment that you saw the Red Bulls in action could swing a negotiation your way, or create a useful connection. It'll also show you're interested in the community and that won't do you any harm.'

Perfectly perfect?

'You make a strong case,' he allowed. 'But here...' He fished out his credit card. 'Charge the tickets to this.' He didn't want her out of pocket.

'But—'

'Legitimate business expenses,' he declared over the top of her protests.

'Oh!' She took a step back and then gestured to what he was wearing. 'I've interrupted your morning run.'

'Just going to hit the hotel gym for an hour.'

She rolled her eyes. 'Flynn, for heaven's sake!'

'What?'

'Look out the window.' She pointed.

He turned to stare, but he didn't know what he was supposed to be looking at.

'The sun is shining,' she said as if speaking to a six-year-old. 'Fresh air.' She slammed a hand to her hip. 'What is wrong with you? If you're going to buy a Munich business the least you can do is breathe in the Munich air.'

Did she know how cold it was out there?

'Instead of some perfectly temperature controlled recycled air that's free of the scent or taste of any-thing.'

There was that word again—*perfectly*.

He thrust out his jaw. 'It's convenient.'

'But is it interesting? Does it teach you anything? Is it fun?'

That last stung.

She shook her head. 'Give me five. I know the perfect jogging trail.'

He opened his mouth to refuse. *Dear Daisy...* He closed it again. 'You jog?'

'Under sufferance. I'll meet you in the foyer in five minutes.'

It took her six, not that he pointed that out as she called a *guten Morgen* to Bruno. An altogether dif-ferent emotion gripped him when he surveyed her legs in their fitted track pants. Addie didn't have a classically beautiful shape—her hips were too wide and her chest too small—but it didn't stop him from wondering what it'd be like to drag those hips against his and—

Whoa! Inappropriate. Employee. Jeez.

'C'mon, we're going to jog by the river. I went for a walk down there yesterday. It's gorgeous.'

It took them three minutes to reach it. She made them go across the bridge and down to the park on the other side. 'See, what did I tell you?'

She stretched her arms out wide and he had a sudden image of her sprawled beneath him, tousled and sultry and—

Why did he have to go and read 'Till the Cows Come Home'? Why did he have to see Addie in a whole new light?

For a moment he was tempted to tell her she could jog on her own, that he was going back to the hotel.

Wish you were here,
Love Buttercup.

He bit back an oath. She didn't deserve that from him. She'd had enough grief in her life without him adding to it. All he had to do was get his hormones in check.

'You really need to get the kinks out, don't you?'

He turned to find her, hands on hips, surveying him. What was so wrong about being perfectly perfect? What the hell did perfectly perfect mean anyway?

'I know it's cold but breathe it in.' She took a deep breath and so did he. 'Can you smell it?'

He knew exactly what she meant. Could he smell the land? Yes. He could smell the brown of the river and the green of the grass and the tang of sap and bark and tree. The air was thinner than home, and colder, but invigorating too. Without another word she set off down the path at a jog.

He set off after her, breathing in the cold air and trying not to notice how her hips moved in those track pants.

She set an easy pace. He could've overtaken her if he wanted, but, for reasons he refused to delve into, he chose not to.

He wasn't sure for how long they jogged, maybe ten minutes, when she pulled up short and pointed to an upcoming bridge. 'Look, it has statues on it like something out of *Lord of the Rings*.'

As they approached he noticed the detail and workmanship. He was about to suggest they go up onto the bridge to discover whom the statues commemorated when she grabbed his arm and pulled him to a halt. She pointed to her right. 'Look at that,' she breathed. 'Isn't it the most splendid building?'

Splendid described it perfectly.

'The first thing I did when I got back from my walk yesterday was find out what it was.'

He really should've done more homework before landing here. So much culture and history just outside his door and he hadn't even been aware of it. *What is wrong with you?* What indeed?

'Do you know what it is?'

A lump blocked his throat and he couldn't have explained why. He shook his head.

'It's home to the state parliament so I guess it should be grand, *but...*'

He understood her *but—but I've never seen anything like it before; but there's nothing like this in Australia; but it's outside my experience and I'm in a foreign country and it's amazing and exciting and an adventure.*

All the total antithesis of the reason he was here.

'Are you okay, Flynn?'

Apparently he was perfectly perfect for all the good it did him. He glanced down at her. The exercise had brightened her cheeks and eyes. A well of yearning rose up inside him. How had she held onto her excitement and joy and hope in the face of all her grief?

'Flynn?'

He shook himself. 'It's just occurred to me that I've been working too hard.'

'One should never work so hard that there's no time for this.' She gestured to the parliament building, the bridge and river.

He made a vow then. As soon as he'd vanquished Mueller, he'd find his excitement again. He'd make time to feed his soul with adventure and joy the way Addie did.

After the meeting with Flynn's lawyers the next day, which Addie had insisted on attending despite Flynn's assurances that she needn't, Addie needed a shopping trip. She'd endured forty minutes of boring, boring, boring. The four men had talked figures and had used phrases like 'projected outcomes', 'financial prognoses', 'incorporated portfolios' and 'Regulation 557' until she'd thought her brain would leak out of her ears and her feigned interest would freeze into a kind of rictus on her face.

The shopping, though, sorted her out.

She let herself into her room, collapsed onto the sofa and grinned at the assortment of bags that surrounded her. Oops. She might've gone a little overboard.

Oh, what the heck? She leapt up and tipped the contents of one of the bags onto the bed. Slipping out of her jeans, she tried on her new outfit and raced to the mirror. 'You'll never believe this, Robbie, but I have a cleavage!'

Her? A cleavage? She grinned, and then grinned some more, literally chortling. She turned to the left and then to the right before giving her reflection a thumbs-up. She'd only ever be able to wear it for fancy dress, but—

The phone rang.

She lifted it to her ear. 'Hello?'

'I need you in here. Right now.'

Flynn. 'But—'

There was no point speaking. The line had gone dead.

What on earth? She glanced down with a grimace, but headed next door without delay. She'd barely knocked before the door was yanked open.

'I...' Flynn did a double take. 'What on earth are you wearing?'

'It's a traditional Bavarian costume.'

'It's gingham!'

'The skirt of the dirndl is gingham,' she corrected. Blue-and-white gingham to be precise. 'The blouse is white and the bodice of the dirndl is royal blue.' Lord, she was babbling, but she could barely form a coherent sentence when Flynn stared at her chest like that. Her hand fluttered to her cleavage in an attempt to hide it. She cleared her throat. 'What's the emergency?'

He snapped to and swore, but he grabbed her arm and pulled her into the room. 'You're not even wearing shoes,' he groaned.

'I can go change.'

'No time.'

She wanted to shake him. 'For what?'

A heavy knock sounded on the door. He moved her away from it with another smothered curse. 'There's no time to explain, but just follow my lead. I need deadpan, no surprise. Cool, smooth and efficient.'

'Roger,' she murmured back.

He planted himself at the table with a file and his computer and then gestured towards the door. 'Please let Herr Mueller in.'

'Herr Mueller,' she repeated under her breath as

she moved to the door. 'Herr Mueller?' she said when she opened it.

A pair of bushy eyebrows rose as they stared down at her. 'Yes.'

'Please come in.'

He took in her attire and twinkling eyes transformed a gruff face. 'You look charming, *fräulein*.'

She smiled back. 'I'm afraid you've rather caught me on the hop.'

'And I've been rewarded for it.'

What a nice man. 'Do come in, Herr Mueller. Mr Mather is expecting you.'

Those lips firmed and the bushy eyebrows lowered over his face when he entered the room. She swallowed and recalled Flynn's demand—cool, smooth and efficient. She gestured towards the table.

'Hello, Flynn.'

'Herr Mueller.' Flynn didn't rise or offer his hand. He didn't ask the other man to sit. He simply leaned back and crossed his legs. 'You wanted to talk. Well, talk.'

Her head rocked back. This was no way to do business, surely? She gripped her hands in front of her. At least it wasn't how he'd done business with her or Herr Gunther or Herrs Schmidt, Schuller and Schubert.

The air in the room started to bristle and burn. She surged forward. 'Coffee?' she asked, hoping to ease the way.

'That would be appreciated,' Herr Mueller said with a forced smile.

'No coffee,' Flynn said with a glare, his voice like flint.

She realised then he didn't mean no coffee for him. He meant no coffee full stop. She blinked at his rudeness and choked back her automatic rebuke. His room. His rules. Fine, no coffee.

She had no idea what to do with herself—where to sit or where to stand. She decided to remain right where she was—behind Herr Mueller. She'd promised Flynn deadpan but now she wasn't sure that she could deliver. At least back here Herr Mueller wouldn't witness her shock.

Flynn would. If he bothered to glance her way. At the moment he was too busy summing up his… adversary, if that was what Herr Mueller was, to pay any attention to her.

'I didn't want to talk,' Herr Mueller said and she suddenly realised that behind the heavy German intonation there was a thread of an Australian accent. 'I just wanted to see your face and it tells me everything I need to know.'

Malice flashed in Flynn's smile. 'Good.'

He was enjoying this? Addie wished herself anywhere else on earth. She'd even plump for Lorna Lee's. In fact, Lorna Lee's suddenly seemed like a very attractive option.

'You're determined to ruin me?'

'I am. And I'll succeed.' The words were uttered smoothly, ruthlessly, triumphantly. Addie stared down to where her toes curled against the plush pile of the carpet.

'You hold a grudge for a long time.'

'Only the ones worth keeping.'

She glanced from one to the other. What on earth were they talking about?

'You may succeed in your aim, Flynn—'

'I have every intention of succeeding, George, and I'll relish every moment of it.'

She shivered and chafed her arms.

Herr Mueller frowned and leaned towards him. 'What you don't realise yet is that in the process you'll lose more than you gain. Are you prepared for that?'

Her head lifted at the pity in the older man's voice.

'No doubt that's what you'd like me to think.'

The older man shook his head. 'Despite what you think, I was sorry to hear about your father.'

Flynn laughed, but there was no humour in it. Herr Mueller turned to leave and Addie did what she could to smooth her face out into a calm mask. He held his hand out to her and she placed hers in it automatically. 'It was nice to meet you, Fräulein...'

'Ramsey. Adelaide Ramsey.' She tried to find a smile but she suspected it was more of a grimace. 'Likewise.' She leapt forward to open the door for him. *'Auf wiedersehen.'*

When the door shut behind the older man she swung back to Flynn, hands on hips. 'What on earth was that all about? My parents would've had my hide if I'd ever been as rude as you just were.'

'You were obviously raised more nicely than me.'

She gaped at him.

'By the way, Addie, you need to work on dead-pan.'

'While you need to work on your manners! That man would have to be seventy if he's a day. Would it really have killed you to offer him a seat and a cup of coffee?' She dragged both hands back through her hair, paced to the door and back again.

Those hateful lips of his twitched. 'I've shocked you to the core, haven't I?'

'I may not know much about wheeling and dealing but that's no way to do business.'

'And yet it's exactly how I mean to conduct myself while in Munich, Addie. You don't have to like it.'

Like it? She hated it.

His face grew hard and cold. 'So you have two choices. Either shut up and put up or jump on the first plane back to Australia.'

She almost took the second option, but remembered her promise to Robbie. *Of course I'll see the world. I'll visit all of the places we've talked about.* The places they'd always meant to visit together. It hit her then, though, that they'd never considered—let alone discussed—what that promise might eventually cost.

When did the price become too high?

'You didn't come here to buy a brewery, did you? This isn't about making some boyhood dream come true.'

He laughed—a harsh sound. 'A boyhood dream? Where on earth did you get that idea? The brewery is only important insomuch as it's currently Mueller's. Make no mistake, though, I mean to take it from him.'

She took a step back. 'You came here with the express purpose of ruining him.'

'I did.'

She stared at him. 'It's Christmas, Flynn.' Who planned revenge at Christmas?

'I told you I was ruthless. And if I remember correctly you agreed with me.'

True, but... 'In business dealings, not personal ones.' And Herr Mueller was obviously personal. Nor had she thought Flynn ruthless to this level. She'd just thought him one of those perfectly perfect people who got everything they wanted with nothing more than the click of their fingers.

But Flynn wasn't perfect. He was far from perfect.

He leaned forward as if he'd read that thought in her face. 'Think whatever you want, but I'm not the Scrooge in this particular scenario.'

Oh, as if she was going to believe that! 'What do you do for an encore—steal candy from babies?' she shot back.

He straightened and he reminded her of a snake readying itself to strike. 'As you haven't left yet I take it you've chosen to put up and shut up?'

Her stomach burned acid. 'Yes,' she said shortly. 'You're right. I don't have to like it, but… Are you sure that man deserves to be ruined?'

He rocked back on his heels. 'One compliment and he completely charmed your socks off. I credited you with more sense.'

The criticism stung. 'He was polite. I was polite back.'

'You were certainly that.'

She folded her arms. 'He seems nice.'

His lips twisted. 'Appearance is everything in these games, remember?'

So he'd said, but it suddenly occurred to her that she might not be the one wearing the blinkers. 'He reminded me of—'

'Let me guess—Santa Claus?'

'The grandfather of an old school friend.' Robbie's poppy. 'A nice old man.' Who'd seen too much heartache.

She walked to the window, blinking back tears. When she was certain she had herself in hand, she turned back to Flynn. 'What did Herr Mueller do to you to deserve this?'

'That's none of your business. And,' he continued over the top of her when she went to speak again, 'for the third and final time—put up and shut up or...'

His *or* hung there like a black threat. She swallowed the rest of her questions. 'Will you need me for the remainder of the day?'

'No.'

Without another word, she left.

CHAPTER FIVE

ADDIE REEFED OFF her apron and pulled the dirndl over her head, leaving them where they fell. She tugged on thick jeans, thick socks and her thickest jumper. She wound a scarf around her throat, seized her coat and slammed out of the hotel.

If she stayed she'd only do something stupid like stride back over to Flynn's room and fight with him. And then he'd send her home.

She didn't want to go home, but...

She buried her hands deep in the pockets of her coat and hunched her shoulders against the cold. Why on earth had he let her go prattling on about marketing strategies for beer halls and import deals that could be struck, huh? She must've sounded like a right idiot! Had he been laughing at her the entire time?

She scrubbed her hands down her face before shoving them in her pockets again. Jerk! Why hadn't he told her the real reason he was in Munich from the start?

Because it was easier?

Because he knew it was wrong and felt uncomfortable about it?

She snorted. He didn't have enough sensitivity for discomfit.

She stomped down the street, but it didn't ease the tension that had her coiled up tight. It didn't answer the question of why her discovery left a hole gaping through her.

What she needed was a long gallop over rolling fields.

Rolling fields. Lorna Lee's.

She slammed to a halt and lifted her face to the sky. She was going to have to spend the next two years working for this man? If she did him some perceived wrong would he then turn on her and try to destroy her? Would she for ever have to watch herself? Bite her tongue?

Ha! As if biting her tongue were a skill she possessed.

She set back off. In her pockets, her hands clenched. She had a feeling it was a necessary PA skill, though, and if she wanted to travel the world as a PA it'd be a skill she'd better master.

She wrinkled her nose. She stomped on for a while longer before thinking to take stock of her surroundings. When she did she came to a dead halt. She hadn't paid much attention to the direction her feet had taken her—other than to stay on well-lit streets. It grew dark early in Munich at this time of year.

This time of year...

Somehow she'd wended her way behind Marienplatz and now she stood on the edge of the square—facing the awe-inspiring Gothic magnificence of the New Town Hall. The enormous Christmas tree twinkled and glittered. The coloured lights and Christmas decorations strung up all around the square winked and danced, and on the balcony of the Old Town Hall a folk group sang a Christmas carol. Beneath awnings the Christmas markets were a feast of sound and scent and movement.

It was Christmas. In exactly one week.

Back home Jeannie would've put up her and Frank's tree. There'd be presents wrapped beneath it in brightly coloured paper. The ham would've been ordered and the Christmas pudding made. Addie twisted her hands together. Frank, Jeannie and her family had shared Christmas lunch and spent Christmas afternoon together for as long as she could remember. She scuffed a toe against the ground. They'd miss her father so much this Christmas Day. Maybe it'd been selfish to come to Europe.

Especially as this would be their last Christmas on the farm.

She scratched her head and rolled her shoulders. It didn't have to be. She could invite them for Christmas next year, couldn't she? Flynn wouldn't mind. Or would he?

She plonked herself onto a bench when a family vacated it and rested her elbows on her knees to frown down at the ground. She'd thought Frank and Jeannie had wanted to leave the farm—it *had* become too much for them—and to move into a retirement village with its easier pace. An email she'd received from Jeannie this morning, though, had left her feeling uneasy. Oh, Jeannie had been cheerful, full of neighbourhood news and Howard's progress with all of his 'new-fangled' ideas, but the cheer had sounded forced when she'd spoken about leaving.

Addie rested back and stared at the Christmas tree. If she was going to be stuck on the farm for another two years Frank and Jeannie could stay with her until they found exactly the right place to move into, couldn't they? She folded her arms.

She'd probably have to get Flynn's approval—he with the noteworthy absence of Christmas spirit and lack of the milk of human kindness.

She ground the heels of her boots together. It wasn't precisely true, though, was it? He'd been kind to her. He'd taken her to the medieval markets. It'd seemed important to him that she enjoy herself. If he truly was ruthless then that didn't make sense.

Did he have an ulterior motive?

She snorted. Talk about fanciful, because, if he did, heaven only knew what it could be.

She bought a mug of *glühwein* and sipped it, appreciating the way it warmed her from the inside out. Back home at Lorna Lee's they'd be sipping ice-cold beer in an attempt to cool themselves. For the teensiest moment she wished herself on the homestead veranda surrounded by people she trusted and understood.

Addie didn't so much as clap eyes on Flynn for the following two days. She'd returned to her hotel room after her glass of *gluhwein* to a terse message on her voice mail informing her that he wouldn't require her services for the next two days.

It made her paranoid. Why had he brought her

to Munich if he didn't want her to do anything? She rang home to speak to Jeannie and Frank, and then Eric, Lucy and Colin. She wanted to double-check that Howard had followed Flynn's directive about Bruce Augustus. She wanted to know that everyone was okay and that nothing dire was going down.

With everything at home seemingly perfect and her fears allayed, Addie went sightseeing. She visited Schloss Nymphenburg—the summer palace of the former Bavarian rulers—where she promptly went into raptures. The palace was the most exquisite building she'd ever seen. But it was the grounds that transported her.

Her jaw dropped as she viewed them from the balcony and her soul expanded until it almost hurt. Formal avenues stretched away, the central one leading down to an ornamental lake with a fountain. Flowerbeds lined the avenues. The colour must be spectacular in spring. Beyond the formal gardens, far beyond, green fields extended for as far as she could see. How perfect they'd be for cantering across, for leaving the cares of the world behind.

She'd spent a long time there—an hour in the palace itself and the rest wandering through the grounds. Did Flynn really mean to forgo all of this in the pursuit of his mean-spirited revenge? There were so many marvels and wonders to enjoy if he'd only stop for a moment and—

Stop it! Trying to understand him was fruitless. He'd have his reasons.

And as he'd pointed out, she didn't have to like them.

She glared up at a sky almost as blue as his eyes and hoped those reasons kept him awake at night.

She visited the Residenz, the palace in Munich— a series of gorgeous buildings and courtyards. The museum of grand rooms depicting differing architectural styles and works of art—paintings, sculptures, tapestries, porcelain and more—blew her away. To think people had once lived like this.

It became a bit too much so she spent the rest of the day in the English Gardens—one of the largest urban green spaces in Germany. She stared at frozen streams and dark green spruce trees and marvelled at how different they were from the creeks and gums back home. She ate bratwurst and drank hot tea and wished Flynn had chosen to join her rather than whatever nefarious plan he was no doubt putting into action instead.

Maybe if he had more fun in his life he'd let go of his grudge and focus on the future rather than…

She snorted. Yeah, as if that were going to happen.

Why are you being so hard on him?

She almost spilled her tea when that thought hit her. Was she being hard on him? She swallowed. Why—because he'd been rude to a man she'd taken a liking to? That hardly seemed fair.

She chafed her arms. No, it wasn't that. It was the hardness that had appeared in his eyes, their coldness when they'd stared at Herr Mueller. It had chilled her, frightened her. She took a sip of tea to try and chase the cold away. Still, wasn't that her problem, rather than Flynn's? He might in fact have a very good reason for his…hatred.

She set her mug down, her stomach churning. That was Flynn's primary emotion towards Herr Mueller. Hatred. She had no experience with it. And she didn't want any either, thank you very much.

Why did he feel so strongly?

She dragged a hand through her hair. The likelihood of finding that out was zilch. She wasn't sure she even wanted to know.

She returned to the hotel that evening to another

terse message from her enigmatic employer informing her that a meeting was scheduled for the following morning and to meet him in the foyer at 9:45 on the dot. 'And let's see if this time you can keep your face halfway impassive.'

She poked her tongue out at the telephone, but raced over to the wardrobe to make sure her little black suit was all in order. Looking the part of the perfect PA might help her act like the perfect PA.

'Good morning, Adelaide.'

Addie leapt up from the chair she'd taken possession of in the foyer ten minutes ago. She'd made sure to arrive early. 'Good morning.'

She bit back a sigh. Flynn looked disgustingly crisp and well rested—perfectly perfect. 'Are you Mr Mather or Flynn at the meeting?' she asked, following him out to the taxi rank.

'I'm Flynn when you address me directly. I'm Mr Mather when you refer to me to a third party.'

She moistened her lips. 'And who might these third parties be?'

He flicked a wry glance in her direction. 'Herr Mueller and his lawyers.'

So they were meeting with the big guns.

'Is that going to be a problem for you?'

She didn't flinch at his sarcasm. 'I don't care what you say or threaten me with, I'm not going to be rude, Flynn.'

The words shot out of her, unrehearsed. She stiffened and waited for him to turn with those eyes and freeze her to the spot. Instead his lips twitched as he opened the cab door for her. 'Try, at least, to keep your shock in check.'

She scooted across to the far seat. 'I've had time to prepare,' she assured him.

Those blue eyes of his rolled a fraction. 'I'm hoping you won't have to say anything at all.'

Fingers crossed.

He remained silent after that. He didn't ask what she'd done for the last two days and she didn't ask him. Who knew five minutes could take so long? She spent the time practising being impassive and keeping her fingers *lightly* clasped in her lap.

They emerged from the cab and she recognised the offices of Flynn's legal team. They were on his turf, then. She smoothed a hand down her hair. How exactly did he mean to ruin Herr Mueller? How did one go about bankrupting someone? She had no idea. It wasn't something they'd taught at secretarial college—at least, not during the brief time she'd attended. Mind you, she could count all the ways disaster could strike at Lorna Lee's—drought, flood, a worldwide drop in beef prices, an outbreak of foot and mouth disease. Flynn, she supposed, planned to be Herr Mueller's natural disaster.

'Addie?'

She half tripped up a step. 'Yes?'

'Tell me your role today.'

She pulled in a breath, eyes to the front. This man had bought Lorna Lee's and was going to expand it in exciting ways. He'd offered her incentives and bonuses to stay—a generous wage and the promise of international air travel. He'd brought her to Munich, he'd taken her to Christmas markets and he'd helped her to shop. She owed him some measure of loyalty. 'My role today is lackey—super-efficient PA and lackey. When you say jump I ask how high.'

'And?'

Oh! 'And I will do my best to keep a straight face, keep my thoughts to myself and to follow your lead.'

'Excellent.'

She followed him into the building with a sigh and tried to stop her shoulders from sagging. It all sounded perfectly perfect. As long as she could pull it off.

During the first twenty minutes of the meeting, Addie learned precisely how to bankrupt a man. What one did was buy out from beneath him the building he'd leased for the last eighteen years and had spent a ludicrous amount of money improving, with the sole intention of not leasing the building back to him. Apparently a verbal agreement had existed between the deceased owner and Herr Mueller for Herr Mueller to buy the premises at a reduced price, but there was nothing in writing. Likewise, all of the equipment that Herr Mueller had spent so much money investing in was now considered part of the premises—owned by the estate and not by him.

'I had a verbal agreement with Herr Hoffman that this building would be mine!' Herr Mueller slammed a hand down to the table.

'Present the documentation to support your claim and I will gladly cede the tender to you.'

She swallowed. Dear Lord, Flynn sounded controlled and deadly.

'It was a gentleman's agreement.'

'Herr Mueller, I don't for one moment believe you a gentleman.'

Addie nearly swallowed her tongue. How on earth did Flynn expect her to keep her face unreadable when he said things like that?

'As far as I'm concerned that building is up for grabs to the highest bidder.'

No points for guessing who the highest bidder would prove to be. She bit her pen, glancing from one man to the other.

'You have no love for German culture! What do you know about brewing techniques or—?'

'I know how to turn a profit. If you want the premises all you need to do is outbid me.'

That cold hard smile! She tried not to flinch.

The only hope she had of keeping her promise was to think of something else. To tune out of the conversation while keeping her ears pricked in case Flynn called her name. She pulled her notepad towards her.

Think, think, think! What was something that bored her to tears? She'd maintain a veneer of impassivity if she were bored to tears.

Artificial insemination!

She wrote that at the top of the page. In the last couple of years there'd been developments in the techniques used for the artificial insemination of breeding stock. Not to mention the collection of bull semen. She bit back a sigh. It could be hard work inseminating a herd of twitchy heifers. Her record was four hundred and eighty-seven. In a single day. Her arm—her whole body—had been aching by the end of it. But, with an injection of funds maybe they'd be able to explore the newer methods.

They might prove quicker. She tapped the pen against her chin. Would they prove as successful, though? She jotted down some pros and cons. She'd need to do some intensive research, check a few websites and talk to some people in the industry. She scrawled down a few names, added a couple of websites to the list.

She bit the end of her pen. The improvements at Lorna Lee's didn't have to be confronting or intimidating. They could be exciting. Think what Flynn's injection of capital could do for the place. They'd be able to increase their output. A smile built through her when she thought of all of the sweet spring and autumn calves they could have. Calving was her favourite time of year.

Who knew? Maybe in a couple of years they'd really start to make a significant mark on the Australian stage. Lorna Lee's had a good reputation, but it couldn't compete with the bigger stud farms.

Not yet. But if they could win a ribbon—a blue ribbon—at the Royal Easter show, Sydney's biggest agricultural show, then interest in their stock and breeding programmes would increase tenfold.

She imagined standing there, holding the halter of a magnificent bull—one of Bruce Augustus's grandbabies—as a blue ribbon was placed across his back. What a moment that would be.

Flynn glanced across at Addie when the lawyers started droning on about ordinances, injunctions and directives. His lips twitched at the dreamy expression she wore. It was a thousand times better than her indignation and disapproval, and it warmed something inside him. He'd missed her vigour and enthusiasm over the past two days. His smile widened when she started to slouch in a most un-PA way, her chin resting on her hands. What on earth was she thinking about?

He glanced at her pad, edged it around so he could read the notes she'd made. She didn't even notice, too deep in her daydream or whatever it was. He read what she'd jotted down and almost choked. He had to hide his mouth momentarily behind his hand. Artificial insemination? He coughed back a laugh. What crazy notion made her think she wanted to be a secretary or personal assistant instead of working at Lorna Lee's?

He nudged her. She immediately straightened.

He rose. She shot to her feet, gathering notebook and pens and slipping them into her briefcase.

'Gentlemen.' He glanced at the lawyers. 'You can stay to thrash this out to your hearts' content, but my resolution is fixed. Unless Herr Mueller can offer a higher bid on the property than I can, I will be buying it.'

This was supposed to be the day of his greatest triumph and all he could think about was taking Addie to lunch and listening to her sightseeing adventures.

'So you're serious in your intent, Flynn?' George Mueller said. There was no desperation in his eyes, only sadness.

'Deadly serious.'

Again, no triumph. The thing was…Mueller did look a lot like…well, Santa Claus. Flynn hardened his heart, deliberately reminding himself what the other man had done to his father. Without another word he turned and left, aware of the click-click of Addie's heels as she followed him.

When they reached the street he didn't hail a cab, but turned left in the direction of their hotel. He glanced at Addie, who kept easy pace beside him. 'Artificial insemination?'

She grimaced. 'I was trying to think of something that would help me keep my face straight, would help me look calm and bored.'

It hadn't succeeded, but he didn't tell her that. Inattentive was a hell of a lot better than 'shocked to the soles of her feet'. He still remembered her flinch when he'd told George that he didn't consider him a gentleman. It had been an almost physical rebuke.

It irked him that she thought so badly of him.

And it irked him that *that* irked him.

They needed to talk. He gestured her into a coffee shop.

'A debrief?' she asked.

'Something like that.'

He moved to a table, but Addie walked right up to the counter to peer at the cakes and sweets on display. 'Ooh, look at all of that!'

'Would you like something to eat?'

'You bet.'

And again she made him grin. Effortlessly.

'I'm on a mission to try every German delicacy I can.' She ordered a cappuccino and apple strudel with cream. After a moment's hesitation Flynn did the same.

'So?' She sat and folded her hands on the table. 'What do you need to debrief me about?'

There was no point beating about the bush. 'Howard isn't taking too kindly to you checking up on him.'

She laughed. 'The others are razzing him, huh? Good for them.'

Their order arrived and he swore her mouth watered as the strudel was placed in front of her. She lifted her spoon and took a bite. 'So good,' she moaned.

He followed her lead. Hell, yeah, it was better than good.

She took a second bite. 'But you can tell Howard not to get his knickers in a knot. I wasn't checking up on him. I was checking up on you.'

He choked on apple and pastry. When she slapped him on the back she did it so hard he almost face-planted the table. He glared at her. 'Me?'

She shrugged and ate more strudel.

'You want to explain that?'

'Not really. You won't like it.' She set her spoon down with a clatter and folded her arms. 'But I can see you're going to insist.'

Too right.

Her eyes—the expression in them—skewered him to the spot. 'I might've agreed when you said you were ruthless, but I didn't believe it. Not really.' She blew out a breath and shrugged. 'You were sort of ruthless in getting your own way about me staying on at Lorna Lee's, but you did sweeten the deal.'

Exactly.

'It wasn't until I saw how emotionless and cold and...hateful you were towards Herr Mueller that I believed it.'

She was right. He didn't like it.

'And then you said I wasn't needed for the last two days and it got me wondering if...'

'What?' He shoved apple strudel and cream into his mouth in the hope it would rid him of the bad taste that coated his tongue.

She waited until he'd finished eating before speaking again. 'It made me wonder if there was some deeper game you were playing with me and Lorna Lee's.'

His stomach churned.

'I started thinking you might've wanted to get me away from the place for a while.'

That was what she now thought of him? He pushed his plate away.

'I thought you might have something devastating planned and didn't want me there when it happened.'

He leaned towards her. 'Addie, Lorna Lee's is mine. Once the cooling-off period is over I can do with it whatever I darn well please.'

'In another three and a half weeks.'

Was she counting down the days? He sat back. 'Why would I jeopardise our contract like that?'

'You're a man who likes to get his own way.' She sipped her coffee. 'You told me yourself that you don't like to wait when you want something.'

'We all like getting our own way, there's nothing unique about that, but why would I ask you to stay at the farm if I was going to do something to it that would get you offside?'

'Because you are ruthless.' She set her cup down. 'And I don't doubt for a moment that you think you know better than me.'

He stared at her. His ruthlessness had really shocked her, hadn't it? It had made her question his entire ethos.

He fingered the carved wooden figure in his jacket pocket. He'd carried it around with him for the last two days. He pulled it out now and set it on the table between them. 'I bought this for you as a symbol of our verbal contract about your bull, Bruce Augustus.'

She reached out and picked it up, turned it over in her fingers. 'It's beautiful.'

He recalled the warmth that had spread through him when she'd told him she believed him a man of his word. She didn't now, though. Now she thought him some kind of power-hungry, revenge-driven monster. 'I'm ruthless only where Herr Mueller is concerned.'

She glanced up. She opened her mouth, but closed it again, her eyes murky and troubled. He recalled the way he'd told her it was none of her business.

He swore under his breath. Addie didn't flinch at that. She didn't even blink. Bred to country life, she was used to swearing and expletives. What she wasn't used to was explicit rudeness. And hate.

'Herr Mueller destroyed my family.' He hadn't known he'd meant to utter the words until they left him.

Her jaw dropped. 'How?'

He dragged a hand across his nape. 'He and my father were business partners. They owned a pub in Brisbane.' Bile burned his stomach. 'Unfortunately you're not the only person to find him charming and benevolent. My father thought the same. That's the thing about conmen, Addie. They're plausible. It's a trick of the trade—that along with their charm.'

She gripped the carving in her hand and held it to her chest. 'What happened?'

He convinced my father to invest all of his money in their enterprise and then fleeced him of the lot.'

'But…but that's awful!'

'He sold up, made a killing and came to Germany, where his father's people were.'

'And your father?'

'He killed himself.'

Her hand reached out to cover his. 'Oh, Flynn.'

She didn't say anything else. Probably because there wasn't anything else to say.

'After that my mother became bitter.'

'How old were you when your father…?'

'Twelve.'

Her hand tightened about his. 'That's criminal!'

'Exactly.' He removed his hand from hers before he did something stupid like clasp it, hold it and not let it go. 'And while I don't have the proof to put him in jail where he belongs, I can ruin him.'

He clenched his hand. 'And I will.' And he'd show no mercy.

'I meant...' She swallowed. 'What Herr Mueller did is dreadful but... It was a terrible thing, your father leaving you and your mother alone like that.' She moistened her lips. 'I know money is important, but people are more important.'

A fist tightened inside Flynn's chest. 'He thought he'd failed us. The man he'd looked up to almost as a father had betrayed him. It was all too much.' His father had become a shadow, a wraith.

He dragged a hand down his face, remembering his father's attempts to explain the situation to him and his mother. He recalled her tears and the drawn, haggard lines that had appeared on her face. His father's pallor and hopelessness had burned itself onto his soul. Those things still had the power to scorch him, to shrivel what small amount of contentment he reached for. George Mueller was responsible for that.

He glanced across at her and tried to find a smile. 'Addie, my father had been so full of life. My mother was always a difficult woman, but when my father came home in the evenings he made everything better. He'd make us laugh and make everything seem carefree and merry and full of promise.' When his father had died, life had never been the same again and it was time for Herr Mueller to pay.

'Why didn't your father fight? Take him to court?'

'Mueller was too clever. He didn't leave a paper trail and he left the country before we'd even realised it. Hell, Addie, he used to come around for dinner. He'd laugh and joke and act like one of the family.' His twelve-year-old self had loved George Mueller. 'But he left without a single word of goodbye. The financial records at the bar were destroyed by fire.' Nothing had gone right for his father. 'There was nothing my father could do.'

'I'm sorry, Flynn.'

He shook his head. 'I didn't tell you this for your sympathy.' Though he knew her sympathy was real. 'I told you so you'd understand my attitude towards that man. So you'd understand why I can't let him profit from my family's misery.'

She nodded, but he could tell she didn't understand. Not really. Addie had experienced grief, but not hatred. In her world one let bygones be bygones. And he couldn't help but be glad of that.

Addie pulled her strudel back towards her. She'd lost her appetite completely, but she could tell Flynn wanted them back on an even footing—didn't want her making a fuss. She understood that. She'd appreciated her friends' and neighbours' condolences when her father had passed, but it had grown old hat real quick too. She realised she still held the carving of Bruce Augustus tightly clenched in her hand. She set him down on the table by her plate. 'Thank you for my carved Bruce Augustus.'

'I thought you'd like him.'

'I appreciate what it represents more.' She pulled in a breath. 'I do trust that you don't mean harm to Lorna Lee's. I do trust that you'll keep your word.' She did trust that he wouldn't hurt her the way—

She cut that thought dead in its tracks.

'That means a lot to me, Addie.'

She believed that too. And that seemed the strangest thing of all.

She spooned strudel into her mouth, made herself chew and swallow. 'Can I be nosy for a bit?' She wanted to get rid of the tight, hard look around his eyes and mouth.

'You can try.' But he said it with the hint of a smile that gave her the courage to persist.

'It's just that I thought you'd grown up on a cattle station, that you'd grown up with money. Now obviously that's not the case. So how did you get from there to here?' To think she'd thought everything had simply fallen into his lap in a perfectly perfect fashion. How wrong she'd been.

'After my father died my mother moved us to Bourke to be nearer her sister.'

Bourke was a small township in the far west of New South Wales. It must've been quite the culture shock to the Brisbane boy.

'In my teens I started doing a bit of jackarooing during the school holidays and on weekends and found I had a knack for it.'

She'd never believed for a moment that hard body of his came from hours spent in the gym.

'I also discovered a talent for the rodeo circuit. I started with camp drafting and breakaway roping and progressed to bareback bronc and bull riding.'

Bull riding? Whoa! Now that was tough.

'You can make a pretty packet on the rodeo circuit. I saved up and by the time I was nineteen I'd bought a small property. I made improvements to it using my own blood and sweat and then sold it for twice the price. Rinse and repeat. At the same time I did a business course by correspondence, made a couple of investments that paid off.'

She stared at him. 'So you're really the epitome of the self-made man.' The twice-married self-made man. What had *that* been about? Not that she had any intention of getting that nosy.

It was none of her business.

And she had no intention of thinking about Flynn in *that* way.

'Once all of this is over, Addie, I mean to draw a line under the whole affair and concentrate on living the life I want.'

A niggle of unease shifted through her. She wasn't convinced that hate could be dealt with so easily. What was more, something about Flynn's story didn't ring true. Not that she thought he was lying. She didn't doubt that he believed all he'd told her, but...

She couldn't put her finger on it. Just that something didn't feel right.

'And what is the life you want?'

'Maybe I'll decide to turn Lorna Lee's into one of the world's most renowned stud properties.'

That'd keep him out of trouble.

He pushed his plate away and met her gaze with a defiant glare. 'I'm going to make my home at Lorna Lee's.'

Really?

'And...'

'And?'

He shook his head and leant back. 'Somewhere along the way, Adelaide Ramsey, you fired me with your enthusiasm. I want to create a successful brewery business here in Munich. I want my beer hall to be one of the best.'

Her jaw dropped. 'No?'

'Yes.'

He grinned at her. She grinned back. 'Flynn, what are your plans for Christmas Day?'

His nose curled. 'Spare me, Addie. As far as I'm concerned, it's just another day.'

She'd bet he hadn't had a proper Christmas since he was twelve years old. She shook her head. 'Wrong answer.'

CHAPTER SIX

FLYNN LEANED BACK, his face an interesting mix of conflicting emotions—politeness and an evident desire not to hurt her feelings battled with bull-headed stubbornness and resentment.

Politeness?

Extraordinary that he took such efforts to don it for her.

No, not extraordinary. She could see now it was his rudeness to Herr Mueller that was really out of character.

'Addie, forgive me, but I don't *do* Christmas.'

Just as he didn't do marriage or romantic relationships any more?

She shook herself. 'Ignoring it won't make it go away.'

He blinked.

And she wasn't above using a little emotional blackmail. She leaned towards him. 'I was going to try and ignore Christmas this year, because... but...'

He reached out to still the hand that worried at the carved bull.

She stared at his hand resting on hers. 'But I find I can't.' She glanced up and suddenly it was real emotion and not an attempt to manipulate pity that gripped her. 'I can't ignore it in this beautiful city, Flynn. Christmas is everywhere and—'

'I'm sorry I thought—'

'No, don't be sorry. I'm happy I'm here. It's an amazing place and I'm having a fabulous time.'

'So what's the problem?'

She scratched the back of her head. She glanced down to hide the tears that threatened her composure. His grip on her hand tightened, but she couldn't speak until the ache that stretched her throat had receded.

When she was certain she had herself under control she glanced up and his eyes softened as they searched her face. He lifted his other hand and she thought he'd reach out to touch her cheek. It shocked her how much she wanted his touch, but he lowered it back to the table.

She moistened her lips, swallowed. 'It seems wrong for me to take so much pleasure in all of this, to be enjoying myself so much when my father died only four months ago.'

'He wouldn't want you falling into a pit of depression. He'd be glad to know you were enjoying yourself.'

'What makes you so sure? You didn't know him. You never met him.'

'Maybe not, but I've come to know his daughter and she has a good heart. She does right by the people in her life even when it's at the expense of her own dreams, and she's done it without losing her sense of humour. She's a lovely woman with a zest for life that has taught me a thing or two. It only follows that your father would be a good man too.'

She bit her lip to stop it from trembling, her chest doing a funny 'expand and cramp' thing. She didn't know what to say. 'Thank you.'

'Life goes on and there's no shame in you finding pleasure in that life, Addie. It doesn't mean you don't miss him or wish he was still here.'

'In my head I know the truth of that, but...'

She eased back, removing her hand from beneath his. His touch had sent a swirling, confusing heat dancing through her and she wasn't sure how much more of it she could take. 'This might seem ridiculous to you, but I know I'll miss him more on Christmas Day. Ignoring the day and pretending it doesn't matter or telling myself that I'm not celebrating it this year isn't going to change that fact.'

He pinched the bridge of his nose between thumb and forefinger.

'I suspect you know what I mean. I suspect it's why you don't do Christmas.'

He glanced at her and his eyes darkened.

She grimaced in apology. 'The thing is, I don't see that it's working for you.'

His head reared back.

'I'm not saying this to be mean,' she added quickly. 'Just trying to work out my best way forward.'

'You think it'll all magically go away—the pain and grief and disillusion—if you celebrate Christmas?'

His face twisted as he spoke and her heart throbbed for him. At twelve his life had been turned upside down. She suspected it hadn't been on an even keel since.

Did he think that it would help ease the burn in his soul if he slayed the dragon Herr Mueller represented?

She tried to find a smile from somewhere. 'I know Christmas is touted as a time for miracles, but, no, I don't believe it'll all magically go away.'

She rested her elbows on the table. 'Heavens, though, wouldn't it be nice?'

He stared at her and the faintest of smiles touched his lips and it occurred to her that she didn't see them as perfectly perfect any more. Instead she saw them as intriguing and with the potential to sate some ache inside her. She blinked and forced her gaze away. He'd been married. *Twice.* The gulf of differences that lay between them almost stole her breath. He had all this experience with romantic relationships while she had none.

Well, not precisely none. But she'd had to make sacrifices where romance was concerned, her duty to her parents and the farm coming first. She didn't regret that, but she wasn't going to now go and develop a crush on Flynn. *That* would be stupid.

'So why put in the effort of celebrating at all?'

She shook herself. 'Because if you don't, you're not giving the good stuff a chance to get through.'

He stared at her but he didn't say anything.

'I think it comes from the same place as your desire to bring down Herr Mueller.'

His eyes narrowed. She suspected a more sensible mortal would stop now, but she pushed on. 'It seems to me that you think if you vanquish him all will be well again—justice served and the world put to rights.'

'You don't think that the case?'

'No.' Her stomach rolled. 'But I can't explain why not. I just can't help feeling you'll lose something of yourself in the process. For the life of me, though, I haven't worked out what that might be.'

He brought one finger down to the table between them. 'You think it's wrong to want justice?'

'You don't want justice, Flynn. You want payback.' If he wanted justice he'd have spent his time finding the proof to put Herr Mueller on trial instead of making the money and acquiring the power to destroy him. 'What you really want is to bring your father back, but you already know that's impossible.'

'Addie—' he spoke carefully '—do you really think this is the way to go about convincing me to celebrate Christmas with you?'

Oh! She could feel her cheeks heat up. 'Sorry, I...' How on earth had they got onto the subject of Herr Mueller again? 'So...' She grimaced. 'You knew that's what I was doing—trying to get you to celebrate Christmas with me?'

He kinked an eyebrow.

Of course he had. She lifted a shoulder. 'I was

going to be all pathetic and use emotional black-mail.' She wrinkled her nose. 'Instead I was just pathetic.'

'There's nothing pathetic about grief.'

'Flynn, it's my first Christmas as an orphan.' Awful word! She met his gaze squarely. 'It hurts me to know that my children will never know their grandparents.'

'You don't have any children.'

'Not yet, but I will.' One day. 'And I don't want to sit at home on Christmas Day moping and feel-ing sorry for myself.'

He didn't say anything.

She hauled in a breath. 'So will you celebrate the day with me?'

'I...'

'Something I've learned over the last couple of days is that sightseeing is more fun if you have someone to share it with. Someone you can nudge and say, "Check that out!" and they can say, "I know. Amazing, isn't it?" back to you. Bearing witness together. A friend. I have a feeling Christ-mas will be the same.'

He still didn't say anything.

She folded her arms and glared at him. 'Oh, for

heaven's sake. It's only Christmas. It's not like I'm asking you to marry me.'

He scowled. 'I don't want something all hushed and reverent.'

'Me neither.' She suppressed a shudder. 'I was thinking of something cheesy. The kitschier, the better.' Loud and rowdy. A revel. A party.

His scowl eased a fraction. 'Do I have to buy you a present?'

She feigned outrage. 'Of course you do.'

He thrust out his jaw. 'I bought you that bull.'

Suddenly she wanted to laugh. 'I'm high maintenance. I want one of the dried plum and almond chimney sweeps that abound at the markets and a pair of mittens.'

His scowl vanished and his laugh lifted her heart. '*That* I might be able to manage. Just call me Saint Nick.'

She wanted to hug him.

Heavens, wouldn't that have him backtracking at a million miles an hour? 'Well, Saint Nick, if you're serious, tell me your plans for the brewery.'

Addie and Flynn spent the next morning touring one of Munich's premier breweries.

'Of course, it's five times larger than the Mueller

brewery,' Flynn said as they pushed through the rotating door into their hotel.

Addie crammed in beside him. 'It was all terribly interesting, though. Who knew—?'

She suddenly realised that she was pressed up against Flynn's side as they moved the five or so steps it took to get from the street and into the hotel foyer. She became excruciatingly aware of the hard leanness of his body beside hers, the slide of his hip and thigh, their contained strength, and the firmness of the shoulder pressing against hers. Her thighs tingled, her knees trembled and she stumbled. His arm slid about her waist and he kept her upright without any apparent effort at all, which only weakened her knees further. 'Careful,' he said.

'Sorry, klutz,' she managed, her voice emerging more breathlessly than the moment warranted. 'I, uh...I should've waited and taken the section behind.'

He shrugged. 'We were talking.'

And then the door emptied them into the foyer and they moved apart. Addie busied herself straightening her jacket.

'You were saying?' Flynn said.

She had been? Oh, yes. 'I was just going to say

how interesting I found the brewing process, and what fun you're going to have getting up to speed on it all.'

He shook his head. 'I'll just hire the best in the business to brew the beer and oversee production.'

As he had with her? Her shoulders went back. Did he think she was one of the best in the cattle-breeding business?

Was she? She'd never thought about it before. Surely not? She—

She bit her lip. She had a lot of experience, though, and—

'What on earth is going through your head?'

She shook herself. 'Crazy thoughts. Artificial in-semination.' It had become their shorthand for her daydreaming flights of fancy.

'Well, if you can drag yourself away from such things I think you'll find our intrepid concierge is trying to catch your attention.'

She glanced over to Bruno and waved to let him know she'd be with him in a moment.

'I have an afternoon of email and phone calls—nothing you can help me with,' he added when she opened her mouth. 'A shopping-centre development in Brisbane that I'm investing in.'

Right.

'So you have a free afternoon. Will you be okay?'

Ever since she'd mentioned that sightseeing would be more fun with a companion, he'd been awfully solicitous. Too solicitous She tossed her head. 'Of course.'

'What will you do?'

'Shopping. Just good old-fashioned girly clothes and make-up shopping. I might even get a haircut.' Her fringe was starting to fall in her eyes.

'Do you have plans for this evening?'

'Not yet.'

'Then don't make any. There's something I think you might enjoy.'

She glanced up into the blue of his eyes. She wasn't sure who moved closer to the other, but suddenly they were chest to chest and the air cramped in her lungs. The air shimmered. His hand lifted as if...as if to draw her closer.

His eyes snapped away. He eased back, clasped her shoulder briefly, but even through the layers of her coat, her jacket and her blouse she could feel the strength in his fingers. 'Meet me down here at six.'

She nodded, unable to push out a sound.

He disappeared up the stairs, the breath eased out of her and she sagged.

'Fräulein Addie?'

She snapped upright and moved over to the reception desk. '*Guten Tag*, Bruno.'

'*Vielen dank*. Look!' He held up a pamphlet. 'I think I have found just the place for you and Herr Mather to spend Christmas. Look, here and here.' He opened the pamphlet and pointed.

Her jaw dropped. 'This is perfect, Bruno. I mean, simply perfect!' She took the pamphlet and flicked through it, her smile growing.

'You would like me to book it for you and Herr Mather, yes?'

'Yes, please! Oh, Bruno, you're worth your weight in gold.'

'I will book a car for you too.'

'Gold and rubies,' she declared. She'd have to buy him a Christmas present for this.

'You're most welcome. It was a pleasure. All part of the service. Also, while you were out these arrived for you today.' He handed her a business-size envelope along with a parcel.

They'd be from home! 'Ooh, thank you. *Danke*.'

He beamed at her. '*Bitte.*'

Addie raced up to her room. She recognised Jeannie's handwriting on the parcel, but the envelope had a typed label. She shrugged off her coat, dropped the envelope to the coffee table and tore the parcel open.

Fruitcake! Jeannie had sent her a slab of home-made fruitcake. A great well of longing opened up inside her. How she missed them!

She laughed over the enclosed letters—Jeannie's full of news of the farm and local doings. Frank had enclosed the local paper along with a photograph of a complacent Bruce Augustus as, quote: 'still the farm mascot'. She kissed the photo. Colin had sent her a drawing of a Christmas tree. She propped it up on her bedside table. She folded her arms and beamed. Her dear, dear friends. 'Merry Christmas,' she whispered, realising that a part of her would be at the farm with them on the day.

She turned to the large envelope and laughed when she pulled out a sheaf of accounts. There wasn't even a note enclosed. Poor Howard. He must think her an awful bully. Or, more like, Jeannie and Frank had bullied him into sending them to her.

Later! She tossed them back to the coffee table. She wasn't wasting a perfectly good afternoon on accounts. Not when she could hit the department stores.

* * *

Addie was waiting for him when Flynn strode into the foyer. She leapt up the moment she saw him, a smile lighting her face and anticipation making her eyes sparkle. Something inside him lifted. She looked ludicrously Christmassy in a red wool swing coat, the colour complementing the colour in her cheeks.

He flicked the lapel. 'Let me guess—a bargain-basement buy on your shopping trip today?'

She stuck her nose in the air. 'I'll have you know that there was nothing bargain basement about this particular number.' And then she grinned. 'But I couldn't resist.'

'Good. It suits you.'

Her grin widened and she took his arm, leading him out of the side door rather than the revolving one. But he was no less aware of her now than he had been when they'd stepped into the revolving door earlier. It didn't stop him from hoping she'd keep hold of his arm, though.

Which could be a bad thing.

Or it could be entirely innocent and innocuous.

Yeah, right.

He ignored that.

She stopped when they reached the footpath. 'Right, which way?'

He turned them in the direction of Marienplatz. He glanced down at her. 'Aren't you going to grill me about where we're going?'

She glanced up from beneath thick, dark lashes. Her new haircut somehow emphasised her eyes. His heart slammed against his ribs. He swallowed, but he didn't look away. 'Would it do me any good? Besides—' she shrugged '—I like surprises.'

She probably didn't get too many of those living on the farm. He suddenly questioned the fairness of asking her to stay on as he had. His lips twisted. He hadn't asked. He'd forced her hand. *Ruthless.*

'Also, I like to surprise other people.'

He shot back to the present.

'And so I don't want to spoil your fun either.'

He stopped dead and stared down at her.

She touched a hand to her face. 'What?'

He kicked his legs back into action. 'Nothing. We don't have far to go,' he added to forestall any questions.

He led her across the road and down a side street. 'And here we are.'

She glanced at the building they'd stopped in

front of and her mouth formed a perfect O. 'Where are we?'

'Peterskirche—the Church of St Peter.'

'I visited Frauenkirche the other day. It was amazing.'

He made a mental note to visit it as well. He'd seen the twin soaring towers multiple times, had used them on more than one occasion to orient himself, but he'd yet to go inside.

'Peterskirche is the oldest church in Munich.'

'It's beautiful.'

'My guidebook tells me it's in the Rococo style. C'mon.' He urged her forward. 'We're going inside.'

There were lots of people inside already. He found them a seat about halfway down the nave. 'Are we going to attend a mass?' she whispered.

He pointed to the front. She craned her neck to look and then her face lit up like a little child's. 'A concert?'

'A Christmas concert brought to you today by your friendly Munich Philharmonic.'

She started to bounce. 'A proper orchestra?'

'The best in Munich,' he promised. He had no idea if they were or not, but it seemed a pretty safe bet.

As he'd guessed, the concert proved a hit with Addie. What he hadn't expected was how much her delight would make his chest swell, or how much he would enjoy the atmosphere and the Christmas music for himself. When it was over they just sat there and let the church empty around them.

'Magical,' she finally whispered, turning to him.

'Stunning,' he said, turning more fully towards her. 'I couldn't believe how high those violins soared in the last piece.'

She clasped his arm. 'Or how those cellos could make your chest feel hollow and full at the same time. It was so beautiful I nearly cried.'

He stood, dragging her with him. He didn't mean to. He didn't mean for his arm to slide about her waist either, but she didn't pull away. Her hands rested against his chest. The searing brown of her eyes felt like whiskey in his veins and when that gaze lowered to his mouth he swore he started to smoke and smoulder.

His grip tightened. Her breath hitched and her fingers curled to grasp the lapels of his coat. He wanted to kiss her. He had to kiss her. Kissing her would be like soaring with that extraordinary music.

Hunger and heat filled her eyes. Her lips parted.

He drew the scent of her into his lungs, hunger roaring through his every cell and sinew. His gaze locked onto those lips—so inviting, so promising. He lowered his head until their breaths merged, letting the tension build inside him.

What do you think you're doing?

He froze. Acid burned his stomach.

He dropped his arms from around her, straightened and tried to take a step back, but her fingers still gripped his coat anchoring him to the spot. A breath shuddered out of her and then comprehension dawned in her eyes. She snatched her hands away and tossed her head. 'That's right. I remember—two ex-wives and no canoodling with the hired help.'

She turned, eased out of the pew and headed for the arch of the doors. He set off after her, not reaching her until they were outside. She stood on the steps looking everywhere but at him. A fist tightened in his chest. 'I'm sorry, Addie, that was my fault. I got caught up in the moment.'

She glanced at him and sort of wrinkled her nose. 'Yeah, well, you weren't the only one.' And it made things sort of all right between them again and the fist loosened, though he didn't know how it could, given the intensity of what had just passed between them.

Almost passed between them, he corrected.

He gestured in the direction of the town square. 'You want to go get a bite to eat? Maybe some *glühwein*?'

'Food, yes. *Glühwein*, no. I don't need that kind of heat flowing through my veins at the moment.'

She had a point.

He fell into step beside her. She didn't take his arm. He glowered at the footpath. 'You're more than the hired help, you know?'

'It was just a turn of phrase. I know I'm one of the *most* important cogs in your wheel.'

She'd said it to make him laugh only it didn't. He scowled. She wasn't a cog.

'So tell me about the ex-wives.'

He rolled his shoulders, tightened the belt of his coat and shoved his hands into his pockets. 'Nosy, aren't you?'

'Nosy is better than hot and bothered.'

Ah.

'Besides, you said back at Lorna Lee's that you wanted us to get to know each other.'

Yeah, but he hadn't meant…

He glanced down at her and let the thought trail

off as a new thought struck him. 'It seems to me that you know me better than I know you.'

She snorted as they broke onto Marienplatz. 'How do you figure that one?'

'Herr Mueller.'

'Oh.'

The sights, sounds and scents of Christmas surrounded them. He glanced about and shook his head. It was so Christmas-card perfect it was as if Munich were the very place Christmas had been invented.

'I'll make a deal with you, Flynn.'

He snapped back to her.

'You buy me a hot chocolate—' she pointed to a street vendor '—and ask me any question you want and I'll answer it.'

Deal.

'And then you'll tell me about your ex-wives.'

His hands went to his hips. 'You're getting two for the price of one.'

Her smile widened. 'Ooh, is there a juicy story to be had, then?'

Hardly.

'Tell you what.' Her eyes danced and it was almost impossible to resist her. 'You get the hot chocolates and I'll grab some doughnuts.'

'Whatever,' he muttered. 'Anything for some peace.'

They found a vacant bench and sipped their hot chocolates. 'C'mon,' she ordered. 'Fire away. Ask me a question.'

Fine. 'What I'd like to know is why you're so gung-ho to leave Lorna Lee's, when you obviously love the place, to travel the world as a PA when you obviously find the work as dull as ditch water?'

'Whoa.' She lowered her mug to her lap. 'Now that's a two- or three-pronged question.'

'I'm happy to get a two- or three-pronged answer. Don't forget,' he added, 'you'll essentially be getting two stories from me. Two wives, remember?'

She snorted. 'How could I forget? Two for the price of one.'

He wished, but they'd been far more expensive than that.

'Okay, Lorna Lee's is the only place I've ever known, the only place I've ever lived, other than a few months in Dubbo where I attended secretarial college. I want to experience something else, something wildly different.'

He understood that, but, 'It doesn't necessarily follow that different is better.'

'Maybe. Maybe not. I'd like the chance to find that out for myself.'

He got that too, but what if in the future she regretting burning her bridges at Lorna Lee's?

'As for the PA bit? Well, I might've been wrong there. When you wear jeans and work boots every day the lure of those little suits can be hard to resist.'

She could say that again. She looked great in those little suits.

'I've been thinking about it. I think bar or restaurant work might suit me better.'

It'd be a waste of her talents.

'Or maybe even retail. I like working with people and I like being on my feet all day.'

How come, then, did he get the impression she'd choose Bruce Augustus's company over people's most days?

'It's not the how of it. Just the fact that I get out there and see the world.'

'You don't have to stop working at Lorna Lee's to achieve that. Four weeks' annual leave a year, free air travel.'

She offered him the bag of doughnuts. He took one. She did too and bit into it. The sugar glazed her lips. He stared and an ache started up inside him before he could wrench his gaze away.

'When we were growing up my closest friend and I used to dream of all the places we'd visit once we were old enough to leave Mudgee. We ordered travel brochures and made up itineraries. We'd spend hours at it. We...'

She trailed off and some instinct warned him to remain silent, not to push her.

A couple of moments later she shook herself. 'When we were sixteen, though, Robbie got sick—leukaemia.'

His every muscle froze. Robbie was Daisy!

'We still made our plans. We were convinced she could beat it.'

But she hadn't and his heart bled for the woman seated beside him, the woman who still mourned her childhood friend.

'She died when we were eighteen.' She sipped hot chocolate and stared out at the square, at the crowds and the stalls and the decorations, but he knew she didn't see them.

'Addie, I'm sorry.'

'Thank you.' But she said it in that automatic way. She glanced at him. 'Before she died I promised that I'd make our dream come true. And that's what I mean to do.'

A chill chased itself down his spine. Couldn't she see how crazy it was to focus on this childhood dream to the detriment of everything else in her life? Living the life Robbie had dreamt of wouldn't bring her back. And Addie deserved better than to be living someone else's dream.

CHAPTER SEVEN

'ADDIE?'

Addie glanced up to find Flynn scratching a hand through his hair. 'Yes?' she said, instead of now demanding the ex-wife story. She'd asked for it because she'd hoped it'd cool the heat stampeding through her blood. She'd wanted him to kiss her so badly her fingers had ached with it. She still did.

'I understand how heartbreaking it must've been to have lost your friend.'

She snapped away to stare out at the square with all of its Christmas glory, but the lights and festivities had lost their charm. Did he understand? Really? She thought of his face and how it had come alive when he'd described his father and thought that maybe he did.

It didn't change the fact that she didn't want to talk about Robbie. Not to him. Not to anyone. All of them had tried—Mum and Dad, Jeannie and Frank, even Robbie's mum and dad—but some things went too deep. Besides, what was there to say? Robbie was gone. She'd died far too young. End of story. Nothing any of them could do would bring her back. So she didn't answer Flynn now.

'But,' he said.

She stiffened. But? No buts! She glared at him to indicate the conversation was over.

'But,' he repeated, evidently oblivious to her silent signals. 'How old were the pair of you when you made these plans?'

'What's that got to do with anything?'

'Sixteen?'

'We'd been making travel plans since we were twelve.' He just stared at her. She glared and shrugged. 'These particular plans?' The particular itinerary Addie meant to follow? She shrugged. 'Nearly seventeen.' That 'nearly' mattered. Every single day had mattered.

'You were only children.'

'And, again, what's that got to do with anything? We were on the cusp of adulthood.' And talking about that itinerary had fired Robbie with enthusiasm, with the desire to get well, with hope.

'You made a plan to see the world at sixteen, which you turned into a pact at eighteen. The point I want to make is that you can fit that promise into your life the way you see it now rather than how you viewed it then.'

What on earth?

'Like ninety-nine per cent of teenagers the world over, you dreamed of independence and getting away from school, home and all the usual restraints. What could be more attractive and exciting than descending upon Europe? What you're not factoring in, however, is the way your world is now, the way your life has changed.'

'I'm not sure what you're getting at.' Her stomach scrunched up tight. 'And frankly, Flynn, I'm not sure I'm interested.'

His eyes narrowed. 'Just for a moment let's imagine Robbie had lived. You're both nineteen and about to embark on a working holiday around Europe for a year.'

That wasn't hard to imagine. She'd imagined it a thousand times. It didn't stop Flynn's words from tearing something inside her.

'Before you can leave, however, your mum gets sick and you have to stay at home to help look after her and the farm. Would Robbie have held that against you?'

'Of course not!' How could he even think such a thing?

'Right, so, hypothetically speaking, your trip has been delayed for a year, but during that time Robbie has met someone and fallen in love and she wants him to come on your working holiday too. Are you okay with that?'

It wasn't the way they'd envisaged it. She busied herself scrunching closed the bag of doughnuts, not understanding her sudden urge to hit the man beside her.

'And three months into your trip she falls pregnant and suddenly she wants to go home and marry her guy and have the baby and be near her mother.'

She gaped at him.

'Are you going to hold that against her?'

She couldn't answer him. The lump in her throat had grown too big. She couldn't even shake her head. Even blinking hurt. But...

If only that were true! If only Robbie were alive in the world with a man who adored her and a couple of rug rats.

If only.

She closed her eyes and fought for air. Her lungs cramped but she refused to let them get the better of her. She focused on relaxing them rather than fixing on the pain screaming through her, the sense of loss. Eventually she was able to swallow.

'I would do anything for that to be true, but it's impossible, and talking about it like this doesn't help, Flynn. It's cruel, as if you're deliberately taunting me with what should've been.'

His eyes darkened. 'I'm not trying to hurt you. It's the last thing I want to do. I'm trying to show you that you'd have been prepared to alter the plan to accommodate changes in Robbie's circumstances. If she was half the friend to you that you were to her—'

'Don't you doubt that for a second!'

Her hands fisted. He stared at them and nodded, half smiled. 'The pair of you must've been a force to be reckoned with.'

The anger evaporated out of her on a breath. Her shoulders sagged.

'I'm just saying she'd have been prepared to alter the plan to allow for changes in your circumstances too.'

'What changes?' She whirled on him. 'I haven't fallen in love, no ankle biters, and I still have my health. Nothing has changed for me. Nothing!'

'How can you say that? Your parents died and the entire responsibility for Lorna Lee's fell to you.'

'Not for long.'

He reached out to grip her shoulders and it reminded her of that moment back in the church. The moment they'd both best forget.

'I don't know why you're so hell-bent on hiding from it, but you love Lorna Lee's. You love the breeding programme, the land, Bruce Augustus, Blossom and Banjo and all of the people there.'

'That doesn't mean it's my destiny.' Robbie had never had the chance to leave, but Addie wasn't letting her down.

'Travelling the world won't bring her back, Addie.'

She thrust out her chin. 'Perhaps not, but it makes me feel closer to her.'

His grip tightened. 'And when it's done—when you've visited all the places you spoke about—what then? What will you be left with?'

The question shocked the breath out of her. She had no answer for it. It wasn't a question she'd ever considered. 'I'm not sure that matters.'

'I think it matters most of all. I think if Robbie had lived, and as the two of you matured, it's something you'd have considered.'

Why was he so worried about her, concerned for her? And why did his hands hold so much warmth? She glanced at his lips and moistened her own. 'Are you sure you wouldn't reconsider having a brief holiday affair with an employee—just this once, Flynn?'

He let her go as if she'd burned him. 'Lord, you're incorrigible.'

All of this talk about Robbie had reminded her of the mischief they'd got into. Of course, it was far more innocent mischief than what she had planned at this current point in time. Heat stirred through her. She shifted on the bench. 'The thing is, I like you as a person and I really like your body. I'd really like to…'

His face told her he caught her drift. It told her how seriously she tempted him too. She lifted one shoulder. 'I understand you're not looking for a commitment. I'm not looking to be tied down either.'

Those words didn't ring quite true. She frowned before shrugging it off. 'I haven't…you know… in a long time. But there's no one I'd rather break the drought with than you.' She shrugged again. 'I think we could keep it uncomplicated.'

He stared down at her and temptation raced across his face, desire simmered in his eyes. He cupped her face in his hands and her blood thumped. Would he kiss her?

Instead he pulled her in for a hug. 'Uncomplicated? Not a chance. Addie, I've never been more tempted by anything in my life, but...'

But he was going to say no. Her eyes burned. She blinked hard against the warmth of his woollen coat.

'It won't make the pain of missing Robbie go away.'

No, but it'd help her forget for a little while.

She summoned her strength and pushed away from him. 'I take it that's a no, then?'

He hesitated and nodded.

She pushed upright and dropped the bag of doughnuts into his lap. 'I'm going to go back to the hotel now.' She shook her head when he stood and went to take her arm. 'I'd like to be alone for a bit.'

She didn't wait for him to say anything. She just turned and walked away.

It was still early when Addie returned to the hotel.

She peeled off her clothes and had a shower, but it didn't ease her body's prickle and burn or the ache in her soul.

She drank the complimentary beer and ate the complimentary crisps. The crisps crunched satisfyingly in her mouth, but the beer didn't make her drowsy as she'd hoped it would.

She settled on the bed, piled the pillows at her back and watched television for a while.

Would it be awkward when she saw Flynn tomorrow?

Oddly enough she didn't feel embarrassed or self-conscious about what had taken place between them, or hadn't taken place, more to the point. Men asked for what they wanted all the time. She didn't see why women couldn't do the same. She'd asked a question and he'd said no. End of story.

She had no intention of asking the question again, though. He needn't be concerned on that head.

She blinked and realised she'd lost her place in the television show. She clicked the TV off with a sigh. Her gaze travelled across the room, passed over Jeannie's parcel and then zeroed back. Fruitcake! A taste from home.

She settled on the sofa with a slice, relishing the rich scent of brandy-soaked fruit. Yum! How many times as a youngster had she helped Jeannie make the cake, and the giant pudding that'd be brought out on Christmas Day?

An ache stretched through her. Her eyes burned. She bit into the cake.

After a moment she pulled Howard's accounts towards her. If she wasn't going to sleep, she might as well do something useful.

It took less than a minute to realise these weren't accounting records from Lorna Lee's. She hadn't a clue what they were for. One of Flynn's lackeys from the city must've sent them, but why address them to her rather than him? Was she expected to do something with them? She checked her email to see if any instructions or explanations were forthcoming. Nothing.

She shrugged. She might as well check through them. If anything were designed to put her to sleep then accounts should do the trick.

She glanced down the list of figures, toted them up and frowned. Hold on…

She totalled the amounts again. They didn't add up. The figures in the total columns were pure invention. Money had gone missing—significant amounts of money. Were these accounts for one of Flynn's current business concerns? She reached for the phone and went to punch in his room number when she caught sight of the clock. It was one o'clock in the morning. She replaced the receiver and slid the accounts back into their envelope, tapping it against her chin.

This could wait till morning. She didn't want Flynn jumping to conclusions about the reason why she might be calling at such an hour. Besides, knowing Flynn, this was probably an issue he already had well in hand. She rolled her eyes. Of course he'd have it in hand! He hired the best, remember? Some lackey somewhere would've already emailed him about this.

With that sorted, she slid into bed and turned out the lights. And stared at the darkness and the clock as the night crawled by.

Addie rang Flynn at eight o'clock on the dot.

'Addie, there're no meetings planned. The day is yours to do with what you will.'

No *Good morning, how are you today?* Just crisp, impersonal instructions. 'Good morning to you too, Flynn. How did you sleep?' some devil prompted her to say.

He didn't answer.

'Me? I slept the sleep of the righteous, which, as it turns out, isn't so good after all.'

A choked sound resonated down the line.

'Look, Flynn, I don't want you to think there's going to be a repeat of last night's proposition. It's over and done with as far as I'm concerned and I'm not the type to flog a dead horse.'

Air whistled down the line. 'I can't believe you just described me as a dead horse.'

To her relief, though, his voice had returned to normal.

'Moving on. Yesterday I received a package containing some accounts. They were addressed to me and I thought they must be from Howard, but they're not from Lorna Lee's. I'm guessing they must be for you.'

'I've been expecting those.'

Good, so he knew what they were about, then. 'Can I drop them over in half an hour?'

'By all means.'

She was careful to dress in as unthreatening a manner as possible—jeans and a loose long-sleeve T-shirt. She didn't want him thinking she had sex or seduction on her mind.

They were *very* firmly off her mind. And if that wasn't entirely true then they were very firmly off the agenda and that was almost the same thing. It resulted in the same outcome. No sex.

She bit back a sigh and went to grab a pot of coffee from the breakfast room.

Flynn opened his door two beats after her knock.

He scanned her face. She stared back, refusing to let her gaze waver. 'The coffee smells great,' he eventually said.

'Let me in and we might even have a chance to drink it while it's hot.'

He half grinned and stood aside to let her enter. She immediately moved to fill two of the mugs sitting on the sideboard, but her heart pounded unaccountably hard. Darn it! Why couldn't he be dressed in one of his suits rather than jeans? She handed him a mug, trying to not look at him directly, but, man, he filled out a pair of jeans nicely.

'Addie, about yesterday evening...'

'Do we really need to do this, Flynn?'

He blinked.

'I'm fine with it. If you're not, then that's your concern, not mine. I will apologise, though,' she added, 'if I made you feel uncomfortable.'

'Blunt as usual.' He sipped his coffee. 'Okay, we'll draw a line under last night and—'

'Wait.'

He stilled.

'You still haven't told me about the ex-wives.' She moved to the sofa and sat. 'It was part of our deal, remember?' And she wasn't letting him off the hook.

'You want to talk about my ex-wives now?'

'Sure, why not?' She wanted one hundred per cent proof that he was a man she should stay away from, romantically speaking. He might be one seriously hot dude, but that didn't mean he was the kind of guy she should be fantasising about. The more weapons she had in her armoury, the better, because the longer she surveyed the long-legged, lean-hipped beauty of the man, the greater the yearning that built through her. She wanted it gone.

Flynn couldn't believe that Addie wanted to discuss his ex-wives at all, let alone right at this particular moment. Not with the spectre of last night hanging over them.

Nothing happened last night.

'I mean, you said you had no work on today.'

He'd said *she* didn't have any work on today. It wasn't exactly the same thing.

She kinked an eyebrow. 'And I know you're a man of your word.'

Oh, for heaven's sake! He threw himself down into the armchair opposite. What the hell—it'd do him good to relive past mistakes. It'd remind him not to make those same mistakes in the future.

And last night he'd been in danger of making a

very big mistake. Huge. Even with his gut telling him what a big mistake it'd be, letting Addie walk away had been one of the hardest things he'd ever done.

But he had done it.

And he'd continue to do it.

'I married Jodi when I was nineteen.'

Addie's jaw dropped and all he could think of was kissing her. The deep green of her shirt highlighted the rich darkness of her hair, which in turn contrasted with the amber of her eyes. He dragged his gaze away to stare into his coffee

'That's so young,' she said, evidently trying to get her surprise under control. 'I was way too young—' she tapped a finger to her head '—in here at nineteen to marry.'

'As it turned out so were we. We just hadn't realised it.' He could see now that he'd been searching for the family he'd missed since he was twelve. He'd tried to recreate it with Jodi—the first girl he'd ever become serious about—but it just hadn't taken.

'What happened?'

'We met while I was on the rodeo circuit. She was a city girl doing a stint in the country.' A gap year like that was popular in some circles. 'We mistook lust for love and, believe me, there was a lot of lust, but in the end it burned itself out.'

He glanced across to find Addie had her nose buried in her mug. He shifted on his chair. Perhaps lust wasn't the wisest thing to be talking about with Addie. He cleared his throat. 'It turned out she hated country life. She never took to it. I'd bought the first of my properties but I was still making a lot of money on the rodeo circuit and I wasn't prepared to give those things up yet. We started fighting. A lot. One day she left and that was that.'

'Wow.'

'It lasted all of thirteen months.'

'I'm sorry,' she offered.

He shook his head. 'With the benefit of hindsight I can see now it was inevitable. She's happily remarried with a little girl. We've made our peace with each other.'

'Well, that's something, don't you think? We live and learn. It's the way of things.'

He raised an eyebrow.

She nodded and grimaced. 'Okay, I'll stop with the platitudes.'

'I'd appreciate that.'

She kept her mouth firmly shut. He rolled his

shoulders. 'Besides, I didn't learn my lesson as I did marry again.'

'How old were you this time?'

'Twenty-seven.'

She shrugged. 'Twenty-seven is old enough to know your own mind and have a proper under-standing of what you're doing. I don't see how that's repeating a mistake.'

He scowled. Matrimony was a mistake, full stop.

'Who was she, then? Rank, name and serial num-ber, please.'

He didn't smile. Nothing about this episode in his life could make him smile. 'Her name was Angela Crawford.'

He stared at Addie. She stared back and then pursed her lips. 'Is that name supposed to mean something to me?'

'Crawford and Co Holdings Pty Ltd?'

'Oh.' She sat up straighter. 'Oh! You mean Craw-ford Cattle?'

'One and the same. Angela is the daughter of Ronald Crawford.'

'Who's in charge of...like, everything.'

Exactly. The Crawfords owned one of Australia's largest and oldest cattle empires.

'Wow, were the family in favour of the match?'

He nodded. 'I was Ronald's head stockman for a while. I already owned a decent holding of my own, but I wanted more experience. And Crawford paid well.' It had allowed him to expand his operations too. Crawford had bankrolled a couple of Flynn's ventures—projects that had paid off handsomely for the both of them.

'Angela came home from university and I'd never met a woman like her before. She'd been born and bred to country life, but she had polish and sophistication too that...' That he'd lacked and had hungered for.

'I've seen her in the society pages. She's beautiful.'

He couldn't read the expression in Addie's eyes. Somewhere between last night and this morning they'd shut him out.

'Yes, she was beautiful, but it wasn't just that. I was twenty-seven—I'd met a lot of beautiful women. We...'

Addie leaned towards him, her expression intent. 'You?'

'We could converse on the same topics for hours. I mean, I didn't know about art and music or antiques, but we both knew about cattle and horses and business and she laughed easily. She made me laugh easily.' And that had been no mean feat back then. 'She could make a room light up just by entering.'

Addie's shoulders inched up towards her ears. 'You fell hard.'

'Like a ton of bricks. I couldn't find fault with her.' Not that he'd wanted to. 'As far as I could tell we wanted exactly the same things out of life.'

He laughed.

Addie swallowed. 'Why is that funny?'

'Because, at heart, we did want the same things. She just didn't want them with me.'

She straightened. 'Then why did she marry you?'

'Because the guy she really loved was already married.'

She sagged back against the sofa and winced.

'That's not the worst of it,' he said, driving home nails that would remind him for a long time to come that he and matrimony were not a happy mix. 'The man she was in love with owned the farm that bordered mine. The farm we moved to once we were married.'

Addie had drawn her legs under her but now her feet hit the floor. 'No!'

'She married me to be closer to him. She married me so she would have access to him. It took her two years, but she broke up his marriage and ours. And all of that time she played me so beautifully I never had a clue.'

Addie set her mug down as if she had no stomach for coffee. He didn't blame her. He set his mug on the table too.

'What a dreadful thing to do.'

Yep.

'But, Flynn, it wasn't your fault. I mean, you can't blame yourself for trusting her. For heaven's sake, you loved her!'

Which only went to prove what a fool he was. 'I should've seen the signals sooner.'

'What would that have achieved?'

He blinked.

'I mean, it wouldn't have prevented what happened, would it?'

Probably not.

'It wouldn't have stopped you from being hurt.'

No, but maybe he wouldn't have felt like such a fool.

'Mind you, if I was ever betrayed like that I'd be pretty darn bitter.'

The thought of anyone taking advantage of Addie like that made his gut burn.

'You're being wrong-headed about the marriage

thing, though.' She leaned towards him and he tried to ignore the enticing shape of her lips. 'The whole "I'm not suited to it" stance is just nonsense. The first was simply a youthful mistake that could've happened to any of us if we didn't have good people around to give us wise advice. And the second...'

She shook her head and shuddered. 'You did nothing wrong. You have nothing to blame yourself for or to be ashamed about.'

It didn't feel that way. He sat back and folded his arms. 'It didn't stop my heart from being shredded, though, did it?'

'No,' she agreed slowly. 'And I expect I'm not the girl to change your mind on the whole marriage-stance thing anyway.'

For no reason at all his heart started to pound.

'I'm really sorry she did that to you, Flynn, but you know what? Karma'a a hellcat. Angela ought to be shaking in her designer boots when it comes to call.'

He laughed. He couldn't help it.

'You know, if you married one of these beautiful Munich women that'd make the local government authorities look on your tender with a more favourable eye.'

What beautiful Munich women? The only woman he'd seen in Munich that he could recall in any detail was Addie. And marriage? He must've looked seriously appalled by the prospect as Addie burst out laughing. 'At least the desire for revenge hasn't addled your brain completely.'

He tried to scowl. When that didn't work he tried to frown. Then he simply gave up. 'Enough. Where are these accounts?'

'Oh.' She pulled a sheaf of papers from an envelope she'd thrown earlier to the sofa beside her. 'Did you have one of your lackeys send them to me?'

'Nope.'

'Because they're dodgy.' She handed them to him.

What on earth?

She pulled another sheet of paper from the envelope. 'To the best of my knowledge, these are what the figures should say.' She placed the sheet on the coffee table and turned it around so he could read it. 'Which according to my calculations leaves a shortfall of this.'

Whoa. He stared at the amount she indicated. It was just shy of two hundred and twenty thousand dollars.

She glanced into his face and bit her lip. 'I, uh, figured this was something you'd already be on top of, but maybe not.' She cleared her throat. 'If these records are for one of your companies or, what do you call them—going concerns? Then someone is lining their pockets at your expense. They're cooking the books and not all that expertly either, I might add.'

Addie was a hundred per cent on the money.

She glanced at him again. 'Do you know which of your going concerns these figures refer to?'

'No, but...' He leaned over them, his finger running down the list of figures. There was something familiar about them. A niggle teased at the edge of his consciousness, but it slipped out of reach when he tried to seize it.

'Do you have any idea why they were sent to me rather than you?'

He stiffened. 'Can I see the envelope?'

She handed it to him without a word.

He glanced at the postmark. 'This wasn't sent from Australia, Addie. It was sent locally.' He handed it back to her, a grim smile coursing through him. 'From Munich.'

She took the envelope but, rather than study the

postmark, she continued to stare at him. 'You've worked it out, haven't you?'

He leant back, his hands clasped behind his head. He let his grin widen. 'I have indeed. The reason these accounts are so familiar and yet unfamiliar is that they're over twenty years old.'

She blinked.

'These accounts are from the business my father and Herr Mueller owned. The man is now toast.'

Her eyes widened.

'This—' he lifted the documents '—is the proof I need to bury George Mueller.'

Addie gazed at Flynn and it wasn't a trickle of unease that shifted through her but an entire flood. 'Who would send them to me?'

'He'll have cheated more than just my father. He'll have left a trail of victims straggling in his wake. Someone has obviously decided it's time for karma to pay Herr Mueller a call.'

Addie scratched her head and frowned up at the ceiling.

'How did you so quaintly put it—he ought to be shaking in his shoes?'

That had been in relation to his evil witch of an ex. What she'd done had been...

Desperate.

Yes, and despicable. And selfish, callous and harmful. She deserved karma.

And Herr Mueller doesn't?

Of course he did. If what Flynn said was true. It was just… *If!* Flynn was so prejudiced against the other man she had trouble believing in his objectivity. She had trouble believing Herr Mueller was the man Flynn painted him to be.

'We have work to do today after all, Adelaide.'

She snapped to attention, but her heart sank at the triumph alive in Flynn's face, the satisfaction in his eyes.

'We're going to pay Herr Mueller a visit.'

Yippee.

'Can you be ready to leave in forty minutes?'

'Do you need me to prepare anything other than myself?'

'No.'

'Then yes.'

She went to gather up the accounts, but his hand came down on hers. 'Leave those with me, Addie. I'll take care of them.'

With a shrug she removed her hand from beneath his, hoping he hadn't noticed the way her breath had hitched at the contact. She moved towards the door.

'And, Addie?' She turned. 'Wear that little red number, if you don't mind?'

'Right.'

Man, she hated being a PA. She really, *really* hated it.

CHAPTER EIGHT

THEY CAUGHT A cab to Herr Mueller's brewery. Flynn didn't hesitate when it deposited them on the footpath, but strode straight into Reception as if he knew the place, as if he owned the place.

Of course he knew the layout of the building. She'd seen him poring over the floor plans.

But he didn't own it yet, regardless of how he acted or the expression on his face.

She kept up with him effortlessly. She figured that was a lackey's duty and she at least had the legs for that, although she suspected she didn't have the stomach for what was to come.

Is this how you really want to live your life? Because it didn't matter if she were a PA, a barmaid or a shop assistant, she'd still be a lackey.

She hadn't been a lackey at Lorna Lee's.

You will be now.

She shook the thought off. In a smooth motion she slid past Flynn. *'Guten Tag,'* she said to the woman behind the reception desk. *'Sprechen Sie Englisch?'*

'Yes, ma'am.'

She smiled. Partly in relief, but most because she was determined to keep things polite. Or, at least, as polite as she could. 'My name is Adelaide Ramsey and I'm Mr Flynn Mather's personal assistant.'

A flare of recognition lit the other woman's eyes when Addie mentioned Flynn's name.

'We don't have an appointment, but we're hoping, if it's not too much trouble, for Herr Mueller to see us, briefly,' she added as an afterthought. She'd like to keep this meeting as brief as she could.

The receptionist directed them to nearby chairs and asked them to wait.

Flynn raised an eyebrow at Addie as if to mock her, laugh at her. She simply stared—or rather, glared—back. With something almost like a smile he moved to stare out of the window. So she didn't sit either. She just stood there clasping her briefcase in front of her with both hands and staring down at the green linoleum that covered the floor.

Flynn best not try telling her what to wear at Lorna Lee's or he'd get an earful. *Wear the little red number.* Why hadn't she told him what he could do with the 'little red number' instead?

Because you like the way his eyes gleam and follow you around whenever you wear it.

Oh, she was pathetic!

'Herr Mueller would be delighted to see you now.'

Addie snapped to attention and followed the receptionist and Flynn down the corridor to a large office. *'Danke,'* she said to the other woman before she closed the door behind them.

Herr Mueller sat behind a massive desk, looking as mild and Santa-Claus-like as ever. He gestured them to seats. This time Flynn sat so Addie did too.

'To what do I owe this pleasure?'

She had no doubt whatsoever that Herr Mueller wasn't delighted to see them; that their being here gave him no pleasure at all, but he put on a good front all the same and she wanted to nudge Flynn and tell him this was how things should be done.

Flynn didn't answer him. He merely clicked his fingers at Addie.

Clicked his fingers as if she were a dog!

She gritted her teeth. What on earth had happened to, 'May I have the relevant documentation, Adelaide?' She wouldn't even demand a please or thank you.

Lackey, remember? Impressions of power, remember?

Gritting her teeth harder, she slapped the relevant documentation into his hand. He didn't thank her. He didn't so much as glance at her.

He'd notice her if she got up and tap-danced on the table.

You can't tap-dance. And you have no right to judge him like this either.

She glanced down at her hands. How would she feel if someone had financially ruined her father and made him so desperate he committed suicide? Would she act any differently from Flynn? Twelve years old. Her heart burned. He'd just been a little boy.

Flynn didn't speak. He pulled the accounting records from the file. These were photocopies. The originals were in the room safe back at the hotel. Just as slowly he spread them out on the desk, making sure they faced Herr Mueller.

'These were delivered to my assistant yesterday. As you'll see they're accounting records from the pub you and my father owned in Brisbane back in the nineties.'

Herr Mueller didn't say a word. He didn't blanch. He didn't shift on his chair. His eyes remained fixed on Flynn's face and they weren't cold and hard. She couldn't make out the emotion in them—sympathy, perhaps, or regret?

Her stomach lurched. She had an awful premonition this meeting wasn't going to go as well as Flynn hoped.

It was never going to go well!

Maybe not, but she sensed it was going to go badly in a totally unexpected way...in a way Flynn hadn't planned on. She wanted to urge him to his feet and bundle him out of here.

Ha! As if that'd work.

'These records provide incontrovertible proof that you were robbing the business and my father blind.' Flynn sat back and smiled a grim, ugly smile. 'This is the proof I need to start criminal proceedings against you, Herr Mueller, which I fully intend to do. I'll ruin you and then I'll see you in jail.'

Herr Mueller still didn't move. Addie's heart hammered against her ribs. She wished this were one of those meetings where she had to struggle to stay awake. Where she made notes about artificial insemination or, better yet, irrigation systems. That'd be perfect.

Herr Mueller steepled his fingers and met Flynn's

gaze steadily. 'Your father was an extraordinary man, Flynn. So exuberant and full of life.'

One of Flynn's hands clenched. 'Until you crushed it out of him.'

'I loved your father, Flynn, but I couldn't stop him from self-destructing. If my own father hadn't suddenly fallen ill I'd have stayed to try and help you and your mother, but as it was I had to return to Germany.'

Addie suddenly recognised the emotion in his eyes. Affection. Her mouth dried.

'You ensured you left before charges could be brought against you. Don't try and wrap it up in familial duty.'

'There's an extradition treaty between our two countries, Flynn. If your father had wanted to press charges, he could have.'

'You'd destroyed the records, made it impossible for him to prove what you'd done. For a long time I thought you hadn't done anything technically illegal, just ethically and morally. But regardless of technicalities and legalities, you robbed him of everything he had—convinced him to sign papers he never should have. But these records show proof of evident wrongdoing in black and white. The records obviously weren't destroyed after all.'

'Your father loved you very much, Flynn, and I remember how much you looked up to him. Love, however, does not always make us strong. He would've hated for you to think badly of him.'

Herr Mueller's gaze shifted to Addie. 'It was I who sent you those documents, Fräulein Ramsey.' That gaze moved back to Flynn. 'It wasn't me who was embezzling those funds, Flynn. It was your father.'

Flynn shot to his feet. 'That's a dirty, filthy lie!'

'Son, you have no idea how much I wish it were.'

'You're going to shift the blame to save your own skin? I'm not going to let that happen. We're leaving, Adelaide.'

Addie shot to her feet too, her knees trembling. Herr Mueller gathered up the papers and handed them to her. Her hands trembled as she took them. She briefly met his gaze and an ache stretched through her chest. In them she recognised the same concern and affection for Flynn that coursed through her. *'Auf weidersehen,'* she whispered.

'Good day, Fräulein Ramsey.'

'Now, Adelaide!'

She turned and left.

Flynn didn't speak a single word as they exited the building. She glanced up at him, not liking the glitter in his eyes or the thunder on his brow. Christmas carols spilled onto the street from a nearby store and while it might be the season it seemed utterly incongruous to this moment. She swallowed and shifted her weight. 'Would you like to go for a coffee?'

'No.'

It was too early to suggest a beer. She glanced around. They weren't too far from the English Gardens. Maybe Flynn would like to walk off some steam.

She opened her mouth. 'No,' he snapped before she could get the suggestion out. She closed her mouth and kept it closed this time. He hailed a cab. She climbed in beside him wordlessly. When it deposited them at their hotel she entered the elevator without a sound. She followed him into his room, biting her lip, biting back the questions that pounded through her.

She watched as Flynn's jacket landed on the sofa. His tie followed. He turned, noticed her for what she suspected was the first time since he'd hailed the cab. 'What are you doing here?' he all but snarled.

'Awaiting instructions.'

'Go. Leave.'

She turned to do exactly that and then swung back. 'This situation is not of my making so what right do you think you have to speak to me like that?' She dropped her briefcase and strode up to him. 'And while we're on the subject, don't you *ever* click your fingers at me again. Got it?'

He blinked.

'I know this is stressful for you and, believe me, I'm sympathetic to that, but it doesn't give you the right to treat people like they're insignificant or have no worth. Is this how you regularly treat your employees, Flynn? Because you can't pay me enough to put up with that.'

He stared at her and something in his shoulders unhitched. He nodded. 'Point taken, Adelaide, you're right. I'm sorry.'

So far so good.

He frowned and spread his hands when she continued to stare at him. 'What?'

'You're supposed to add that it'll never happen again.'

A glimmer of a smile touched his lips and something in her chest pitter-pattered. 'It'll never happen again. I promise.'

She found herself smiling. 'Thank you.'

He shook his head and collapsed into the armchair. 'You're really not lackey material, you know that?'

She bit back a sigh. That was becoming increasingly evident.

He turned his head from where it rested on the back of the chair. 'I know you'll have trouble believing this, but Mueller's lying.'

She pushed his jacket aside and perched on the edge of the sofa. His pallor and the tired lines fanning out from his eyes caught at her. 'Let's say that's true and that all we have are some doctored accounts.' His gaze speared to hers and she had to swallow. 'How—?'

'How can I prove it was Mueller who doctored them?' He raked both hands back through his hair. 'Yes, therein lies the rub.'

She shook her head. 'That's not what I mean.' He stilled and glanced back at her. 'I mean, how can you be sure Herr Mueller isn't telling the truth?' She held up a hand to prevent him from going into fly-off-the-handle mode. 'I'm not trying to challenge you. I like you, Flynn. You're smart and you work hard.' She admired that. 'Generally you're good-natured and you've offered me a wonderfully attractive bonus to stay on at Lorna Lee's because you want me to be content and settled there. That tells me, as a general rule, that you care about people. I feel as if we've almost become friends.'

'Addie—'

'No, Flynn, let me finish. I feel you need to hear this and there's no one else to say it. Because of all of the things I've just outlined, my loyalty lies with you regardless of what first impressions I may have gained from Herr Mueller.'

He rested his elbows on his knees, his eyes intent on her face. Her heart hammered, but she met his gaze squarely. 'If you are going to ruin this man you need to be very certain of your facts. I mean, how will you feel in five years' time if you find out you were wrong?'

His jaw slackened.

'What actual proof do you have, Flynn? What your father told you when you were twelve years old? Truly, what do any of us know about our parents' greater lives when we're young? We just love them unconditionally and depend on them completely. We're totally biased.'

He leapt out of his chair and paced the length of the room. 'My father was a good man.'

'I believe you. But sometimes good people make bad decisions.'

He didn't say anything. He didn't even turn. She

moistened her lips. 'Has there been a shadow of impropriety over any of Herr Mueller's other dealings since that time?'

Flynn waved that off. 'If my father had been embezzling funds why didn't Mueller have him arrested? Answer me that.'

'He said he loved your father.'

His snort told her what he thought about that.

She pressed a hand to her brow and dragged in a breath. 'I have another question.'

'Just the one?' he growled, throwing himself back into the armchair.

'When your ex, Angela, betrayed you like she did—'

'She was never mine.'

'When she did what she did, she hurt you and her family and tore another woman's marriage apart so...'

'So?'

'Did you go after her like this and make sure she paid for what she did?'

He hadn't. She could see the answer in his eyes.

'So if you didn't try to get your revenge on her why is Herr Mueller different?'

His face twisted and he leaned towards her. 'He killed my father.'

'No, Flynn, he didn't. Your father killed himself.' Her heart quailed as she said the words. 'That responsibility rests solely with him.'

He stabbed a finger at her. 'He drove my father to it.'

'Maybe, maybe not.' She twisted her hands together. 'It's a big question, a big accusation. Do you really want to get it wrong?'

'I thought you said you were on my side?' His lips twisted. 'Or do I need to pay you more to earn that kind of loyalty?'

She ignored that. He was simply trying to get a rise out of her. 'You know what I think?'

'I can hardly wait to hear,' he bit out.

'I think your anger and your bitterness towards Herr Mueller has provided you with the spur to succeed, to reach a position of power where you can make him pay. But are you sure it's really him you're angry with?'

He leapt up, hands clenched, his entire body shaking. It took an effort of will not to shrink back against the sofa. 'I will get you the proof you need. My father *wasn't* a thief!'

'I don't need the proof, Flynn. You do.'

The air in the room shimmered, but with what she wasn't sure. 'I think what you went through when you were twelve years old was dreadful, Flynn, horrendous. I want to horsewhip the world for putting you through that.'

The storm in his face died away.

'You need to remember, though, that you're not twelve years old any more. Nobody—and I mean *nobody*—can put you through that again.'

He stared at her as if he didn't know what to say. She swallowed and rose. 'Would you like me to leave now?'

'I think that would be a very good idea.'

She collected her briefcase and left, walked into her room and promptly threw herself across her bed and burst into tears.

Flynn glanced up at the knock on the door. It'd be Addie. For the previous two mornings she'd turned up at nine o'clock on the dot to report for duty. He'd given her both days off to sightsee.

Today wouldn't be any different. 'Come in.'

'Good morning.' She breezed in wearing a chic navy suit and bearing the customary pot of coffee. He wondered if it gave her a kick to dress up in her office clothes. She set the coffee on a trivet on the table in front of him. 'Did you have a good day yesterday?' she asked.

'Yes.' It was a lie. He tensed, waiting for her to quiz him about what he'd been doing or ask him if he'd found any evidence of Mueller's guilt yet.

He hadn't.

He thrust out his chin. He mightn't have known much at twelve, but he knew his father wasn't a thief!

But Addie didn't ask him anything. He shifted on his chair. 'What about you? Get up to anything interesting?'

'Oh, yes. I walked out to the art galleries, which was quite a hike. I spent hours there.' A smile lit her up from the inside out. 'I love holidays.'

He stared at her, transfixed.

'I like art but I don't know very much about it so I'm going to learn.'

She was?

'I ordered some books online. They should be waiting for me when I get home.'

'Good for you.'

'And then—' her eyes widened '—I caught a tram back to Marienplatz.'

He grinned. This woman could find fun in the most ordinary things. 'A day of art and trams, huh?'

Her eyes danced. 'And bratwurst and black forest cake.'

He'd have had more fun venturing forth with her. *You're not here for fun.*

'What would you like me to do today? Any letters you'd like me to type and post? Any emails to send or meetings to set up?'

'Nothing's happening at the moment, Addie. Everything is quietening down for the Christmas break. Go out and enjoy the day.' He scowled. While he trawled more newspapers and business reports looking for dirt on Mueller. *All you have to do is ask and she'd help.*

Addie didn't notice his scowl. In fact she seemed totally oblivious to his inner turmoil. She stared beyond him and her eyes widened and her jaw dropped. He turned to see what had captured her attention.

'Snow!' She raced to the window. 'Flynn, it's snowing!' She bounced up onto her toes. 'I've never seen snow before.'

She turned and tore out of the room. 'Addie, wait!' He moved after her. 'It'll be freezing out. Take your coat.' But she was already clattering down the stairs. 'Silly woman. It's only snow,' he muttered.

He trudged back and collected his coat. He let

himself into her room and collected her coat and scarf and then stomped down the stairs after her.

She turned when he emerged onto the street and her face was so alive with delight his grumpiness evaporated. He shook his head and tried to hide a grin. 'Jeez, Addie, you wanna freeze?'

He wound her scarf about her throat. For a moment their eyes locked. A familiar ache pulled at his groin. A less familiar one stretched through his chest. Fat flakes fell all around them; one landed on her hair. He brushed it off before he realised what he was about. Addie shook herself and broke the eye contact. With a shake of his head he held her coat out for her. She slipped it on and immediately moved out of his reach.

Neither ache abated.

She turned back to grin at him. 'You're lucky it's only just started snowing. If it'd been going for a while I'd have hit you with a snowball the moment you stepped out of the door.'

He'd welcome a cold slap of reality about now.

She eyed him uncertainly when he didn't say anything. 'I suppose this is old hat for you?'

He hadn't meant to rain on her parade. 'I've seen snow before. In America. Montana.' He injected enthusiasm into his voice. 'But I can quite safely say I've never seen snow while standing by the medieval gate of a European city.'

She grinned back at him and he was glad he'd made the effort. 'It's really something, isn't it?'

Yeah, it was. He nodded and then frowned. Why did he insulate himself so much from enjoying simple pleasures like these? What harm was there in enjoying them?

'You really don't need me today?'

At the shake of his head, she raced back inside.

Flynn remained on the footpath and noticed the way the snow had started to transform everything—frosted it. Munich was a pretty city and the snow only made it prettier.

'Oh!' Addie skidded to a halt beside him. 'Are you sure you don't need me today?'

She now had her handbag slung over her shoulder. 'Your day is your own,' he assured her. She'd go out and see something amazing, enjoy experiences outside her usual world, while he holed up in his room and—

I love holidays.

Addie's earlier words taunted him. When was the last time he'd taken the time for a holiday? His life revolved around work.

Work and revenge.

But seriously, would a day off here and there really kill him? A week off here and there even?

Addie took two steps away. Stopped. Swung back. 'I'm going to sit in a little café on Marienplatz. I'm going to sip coffee and eat pastries while I watch the square turn white.' She moistened her lips. 'Would you like to join me?'

He should say no. He should... 'Yes.'

She walked back to him. 'You're acting very oddly, Flynn.'

'Maybe I've had too much sun.'

'Or maybe you've been working too hard, but may I make a suggestion?'

'By all means.'

'I think you should put on your coat. It's cold.'

He started and realised he still held his coat. He reefed it on.

'A touch of the sun,' she snorted, setting back off. He kicked himself forward to keep pace beside her. 'Brain freeze more like.'

They didn't speak again until they were seated in an upstairs café. Addie had pounced on a window table. 'We'll have the perfect view of the glockenspiel when it ramps up to do its stuff.'

He glanced at his watch. 'That's an hour and a half away.'

She turned from staring out of the window and sent him a grin. 'I don't know about you, but I haven't anything better to do for the next ninety minutes.' She nodded back towards the window. 'Look how pretty the square is.'

She was right. He leaned back and his shoulders started to relax. Ninety minutes of sipping coffee and nibbling pastries and watching the world go by? It had a nice ring to it.

They made desultory chit-chat over their first coffee. Addie told him about some of the art she'd seen the previous day and how it had affected her. When she asked him about his trip to Montana he told her about the mountains and the big sky country.

It wasn't until they were on their second cup of coffee—decaffeinated this time, Addie had insisted—when she turned to him abruptly. 'I've been thinking about what you said to me the other night.'

His cup halted halfway to his mouth. Which night? He set it back to its saucer.

'You asked me what I'd have left once I'd completed my mission—my promise to Robbie. After I'd seen it all through.'

His heart ached at the trouble in her eyes. 'Addie, I had no right to ask such a question. I—'

'No, your question came from a good place. I just found it a bit confronting at the time, is all. It felt as if you were suggesting I break faith with Robbie, break my promise. I can see now that's not what you were doing. You were saying that it would be okay for me to modify the plans we made back then to fit them into my life now, if that's what would make me happier. You were saying that Robbie wouldn't mind me doing that, that she'd understand.'

That was exactly what he'd been saying. He'd wanted to ease the pressure she put on herself. He'd wanted to bring her a measure of peace.

She gave a soft half laugh, but the sadness of her smile pierced his chest. 'You were saying I could dream other dreams too and that wouldn't mean I was being unfaithful to the first dream or to Robbie.'

'It's natural to dream, Addie, and there's no reason why you can't have two, five or ten dreams.' Hell, she could have a hundred if she wanted.

'By doing that—and please be honest with me, as honest as I was with you in your room after our meeting with Herr Mueller.'

His heart thumped when she glanced up at him, but he nodded.

'If I dream my other dreams, if I envisage a different life for myself now than I did when I was sixteen, am I not letting Robbie down? Am I not being false to her memory?'

'No.'

She stared at him. 'It seems wrong to dream when she no longer can.'

He dragged a hand down his face and forced a deep breath into his lungs. 'Addie, being true to yourself won't mean you're being false to Robbie's memory. You'll only be letting her down if you see that promise through at the expense of your own happiness. That'd make a mockery of all that you and Robbie shared.'

'Oh!' Her jaw dropped. 'That has an awful ring of truth.'

He leaned towards her. 'Because it is true. If your situations had been reversed, would you want Robbie to make ludicrous sacrifices just to tick off an itinerary that didn't hold the same allure or promise for her any more? Of course you wouldn't.'

Very slowly she nodded, but behind the warm amber of her eyes her mind raced. He sat back and waited for whatever would come next, determined to do what he could to set her mind at rest. This woman didn't have a malicious bone in her body. She shouldn't be tying herself in knots over this. She should be running out into the snow with outstretched arms every day of the week—figuratively speaking. She should be living her life with joy.

'You see?' she finally said. 'Our time here has been a revelation.' She broke off a corner of an apple Danish and popped it into her mouth. 'Please, no offence, but I've discovered I don't like being a PA.'

'None taken.'

She shrugged. 'Apparently loving the clothes doesn't mean loving the job.'

He laughed.

She sighed. 'I have a feeling I wouldn't enjoy being a barmaid or a shop assistant that much either.'

'Like I said, you're not really lackey material.'

'Also, if I were working a nine-to-five job here, I'd be staying in the outer suburbs, as that'd be all I could afford, which would mean a commute into the city. That means that at this time of the year I could be leaving home while it's still dark and then not getting home again until it's dark.'

'That's true.'

'I've been lucky. I've had more free days since we've been here than work days *and* I'm in the heart of things. It occurred to me I'd rather visit all the places on my list as a vacationer rather than as a working girl.'

Mission accomplished. 'And experience its delights to the full without other distractions and responsibilities weighing you down.'

She nodded.

He straightened. 'So what's the problem?'

She ducked her head, but not before he'd glimpsed a sheen of tears. In one fluid motion he moved from sitting opposite to sitting beside her. He took her hand. 'Tell me what's really troubling you, Addie.'

She gripped his hand tightly. 'I write to Robbie. A lot. In my diary. I've written to her every day that we've been here. That probably sounds silly to you.'

'Not at all.'

'It makes me feel closer to her. And...' A sob broke from her.

He slipped an arm around her shoulders and pulled her against his chest. She cried quietly and unobtrusively, but her pain stabbed at him. He found himself swallowing and blinking hard.

Eventually she righted herself, pulled out a tissue

and wiped her eyes. He swore at that moment to go out and buy handkerchiefs and to always have one on hand.

She didn't apologise for crying and he was glad.

'I don't want to lose that sense of closeness.' She glanced up at him. 'I'm afraid of forgetting her, Flynn.'

It fell into place then—her single-minded focus. 'Heck, Addie, you're not going to forget her! You'll never forget her. It'd be like trying to forget a piece of yourself. She'll always mean what she meant to you, even as new people come and go in your life.' He cupped her face. 'You don't have to lose that sense of closeness. Sure, write to her about Munich. And about Paris and London and Rome when you visit them too, but you should be telling her about your life—the things that are happening at home and the plans you're making and your dreams.'

And then he let her go before he did something stupid like kiss her.

She blinked. She straightened. 'You know, you could be onto something there.' Then she grimaced. 'Except I can't tell her what my dreams are if I don't know what they are myself.'

He wanted to touch her. He sat on his hands instead. 'So you work out what it is you really want.'

'How?'

That question stumped him. 'Why don't you ask Robbie for her advice?'

She stared at him and then a smile broke across her face. It was like morning breaking over rolling green fields. 'Perfect answer.' She reached across and kissed his cheek. *'Danke.'*

'You're welcome.' Though he had a feeling he only thought the words. He couldn't seem to get his lips to work.

CHAPTER NINE

ON CHRISTMAS MORNING Flynn met Addie in the foyer at ten o'clock as she'd instructed. The moment she saw him she beamed at him. When her eyes lit on the brightly coloured gift bag that he carried, which held three even more brightly coloured presents, she rubbed her hands together. 'Ooh.'

'Will I take that for you, sir?' the concierge asked with a grin.

He handed it over. 'Please.'

'I'd also like to take this opportunity to thank you, Herr Mather.' The concierge—Bruno, wasn't it?—nodded towards the reception desk. A bottle of schnapps and an assortment of chocolates stood amid torn Christmas paper.

They'd bought him a Christmas gift? He shook his head. *Addie* had bought him a Christmas gift. 'Merry Christmas, Bruno.'

'Merry Christmas, sir.' And then his gift bag was whisked away.

'Did we buy everyone in the hotel Christmas gifts?'

'Scrooge,' she shot back, which told him they had.

And then she wrapped her arms about him in a hug. It wasn't meant to be sexy. It wasn't that kind of hug. But it sent the blood racing through his veins and his skin prickling with heat, and it was sexy as hell.

She released him. 'Merry Christmas, Flynn.'

Lord, those eyes! They danced with so much excitement her cheeks were pink with it. Beneath the foyer lights her dark hair gleamed. In that moment he swore that regardless of how hokey a Christmas Day she'd planned, he would not rain on her parade. He would pretend to enjoy every moment of it.

Who knew? In her company there mightn't be any need for pretence.

'Merry Christmas, Addie.'

She slid her arm through his and pressed it against her side. 'C'mon, the car's already here. Let the festivities begin!'

He rolled his eyes, but grinned too. 'Where are you taking me?'

She seemed to grin with her whole body. 'You'll see.'

Their driver—Otto—was promptly handed a

gift of fruitcake and spiced biscuits and wished a very merry Christmas. Within two minutes of their journey starting, Addie had wormed out of him that he was a retired chauffeur whose family was scattered. Driving on Christmas Day stopped him from getting too lonely. Oh, and he was looking forward to a family reunion next year.

Flynn shook his head. She might not be lackey material but she had a way with people. It wouldn't hurt him to take a trick or two from her book and apply it to his business life.

For the next hour, they drove in what Flynn calculated to be a roughly southerly direction. They passed through the outer suburbs of Munich until they'd left the city behind, advancing through smaller towns and villages. When they came to a town bordering a large lake, Otto stopped so Addie could admire it. She leapt out of the car and then just stood there. 'It's so beautiful,' she breathed.

Flynn stared down at her, evidently trying to memorise the view. 'Yes,' he agreed. Very beautiful.

'The landscape here is so different from home. I...' She flashed him a grin and then opened her mouth in a silent scream of delight. 'I can't believe I'm here!'

He held the door open for her as she slid back into the car, fighting the growing overwhelming urge to kiss her. Kissing her would be a bad thing to do.

Why was that again?

He scratched his head. Um…

Addie thumped his arm and pointed out of the window as the car climbed an incline. 'Look! It's a whole forest of spruce and pine and Christmas trees! It's like something from Grimm's fairy tales.'

She was right. They were surrounded by Christmas trees. He sucked in a breath. They were going to end up in the great hall of some castle, weren't they? There'd be a roast pig with an apple in its mouth and mulled wine. An oompah band would be playing and carollers would be carolling and everything would be picture-postcard perfect. *That* was where she was taking him.

His shoulders started to slump. All of it would highlight how far short his own Christmases had fallen ever since his father had died.

He passed a hand across his face, glanced across at Addie and pushed his shoulders back. He would not ruin this day for her. He'd enter into the spirit of the thing if it killed him.

'Are you ready, Ms Addie?' Otto rounded a curve in the road and as the forest retreated the view opened out. Flynn's jaw dropped. Otto pulled the car over to the verge. Addie's hand on Flynn's arm urged him out of the car. He obeyed.

'Oh, wow!' she murmured, standing shoulder to shoulder with him. 'I don't think we're in The Shire any more, Mr Frodo.'

Flynn smiled at her *Lord of the Rings* reference, but she was right. All around them soared spectacular snow-covered mountains. Dark forests dotted the landscape here and there along with sheer cliff faces. It all glittered and sparkled, fresh and crisp in the cold sunlight. He drew air so clean and fresh into his lungs it almost hurt. 'This is spectacular.'

'The Alps,' she said, somewhat unnecessarily. 'That's where I'm taking you for Christmas, Flynn.'

He thought of the cheesy medieval castle he'd conjured in his mind. It could still eventuate. He glanced down at her. 'Perfect,' he said. And then he blinked. 'What? To the very top?'

She laughed and pushed him back towards the car. 'All will be revealed soon enough.'

Fifteen minutes later they entered a town full of chalets and ski shops. 'Garmische-Partenkirchen,' Addie announced proudly. 'Try saying that five times without stopping.'

He frowned. 'The name's familiar.'

'The winter Olympics have been held here.'

'Of course!'

There wasn't a medieval castle in sight. She took him to a chalet. 'We're going to dine with twenty-four select guests on one of Germany's finest degustation menus.'

His mouth watered.

'I have a feeling there won't be a mince pie or plum pudding in sight.'

He glanced down at her. Wouldn't she miss those things?

'And there'll be a selection of wines from the Rhone Valley.'

Better and better. He took the proffered glass of schnapps from a waiter.

Addie did too and then she leaned in closer. 'We've been living on bratwurst, pork knuckle, sauerkraut and apple strudel. I thought it time we tried something different.'

Really? Did she really prefer this to a medieval castle?

They were led into a long room with an equally long picture window that looked out over those glorious soaring alpine scenes. They were both quiet as they surveyed the panorama.

'What made you choose this?' He turned to her.

It was suddenly important to know why. She hadn't done this just because she'd thought it was what he'd prefer, had she? His hand clenched about his glass of schnapps. He didn't want her to make those kinds of sacrifices for him.

Her brow creased. 'You don't like it?'

'I love it.'

Her brow cleared. 'When I looked into all the options available I initially started with traditional, but...' She stared down into her glass. 'Well, you see, Jeannie sent me some fruitcake from home and I suddenly realised that if I went traditional I'd spend most of the day missing them.'

She glanced up and the expression in her eyes skewered him to the spot.

'I knew I'd spend the day grieving for my father and I figure I'm already missing him enough as it is.'

Question answered. He pulled her in for a light hug. She rested against him for a moment and he relished it. When she pushed away from him he let her go again. He didn't want to, but he did it all the same.

'I don't mean to ignore it, though,' she said. She tipped her glass towards him. 'To absent friends. To my parents and your father and Robbie.'

He tilted his glass. 'To absent friends.'

She straightened. 'Now, I wouldn't advise you to imbibe too freely of the wine as the day doesn't end with the meal.'

He laughed, but he didn't pester her for details. He'd let the day unfold at the pace Addie had planned for it. And he'd enjoy every moment.

The meal was amazing. They sat at a table for six with a French businesswoman, her Austrian ski-instructor husband and a retired British couple from Bristol. Everyone was in greatest good humour. The wine flowed and the conversation flowed even faster. The food was amongst the best Flynn had ever sampled.

By three o'clock he swore he couldn't fit another morsel in. Not one of the petits fours or another sip of dessert wine. He turned down the brandy. So did Addie. 'I'm sure I say this every Christmas,' she groaned, 'but I have never been so full in my entire life and I swear I'm not going to eat for a week.'

They'd moved into the adjoining lounge area—a room of wood panelling, comfy sofas and a roaring fire. A picture window provided the perfect views of snow-covered mountains and ski runs. Some guests had remained talking in the dining room, some had moved in here with him and Addie, while others had adjourned to the rooms they had booked in the chalet.

Flynn collapsed onto a sofa, slumping down into its softness. He could suddenly and vividly imagine spending a week in the Alps with Addie.

He promptly shook himself upright. Crazy thought!

A bell sounded. People rose. He glanced at Addie and she grinned back. 'Are you too full to move?'

He shook his head. He'd actually been contemplating the pros and cons of braving the cold for a walk.

'Excellent. Phase Two begins.'

'Please tell me it doesn't involve food.'

'No food.'

Two small mini-buses were parked at the front of the chalet. He and Addie were directed to one of them. They drove for three minutes before pulling up again. 'We could've walked,' he said as they disembarked.

'Ah, but we may in fact appreciate the ride home later.'

He stared at the building in front of them and then swung to her. 'This is the Olympic centre. Are we getting a tour?' That'd be brilliant!

'In a manner of speaking. We get to test the facilities out.'

What was she talking about?

She laughed and urged him forward. 'We're going ice-skating, Flynn.'

They had a ball. After a mini-lesson, they were left to their own devices. They fell, a lot, but he still figured that he and Addie picked it up pretty quickly.

'I'm going to be black and blue,' he accused her, offering his hand to help her up after another spill.

'Go on, admit it, you're having fun.'

'I am.' He held her hand a beat longer than he should have. He forced himself to let it go. He gestured around the ice-rink stadium. 'This was an inspired idea, Addie.'

'It's my one gripe with Christmas,' she said. 'There's never enough physical activity, and when I eat that much I need to move.' She glanced at him. 'You're like me in that regard—you like to jog every day, et cetera. So I figured you'd appreciate a bit of exercise too.'

She was spot on.

'Watch this.' She performed a perfect, if somewhat slow, pirouette. 'Ta-da!'

'You're obviously destined to become a star.'

She laughed and moved to the railing for a rest. 'I'm glad you've enjoyed it. I'd hoped you would. You see, the second bus went skiing.'

Skiing!

'And snowboarding.'

Snowboarding!

'And doesn't that sound like a whole trailer-load of fun?'

It did.

'But, of course, the weather conditions couldn't be guaranteed and if visibility had been poor the skiing would've been cancelled. This seemed the safer option.'

'The skating's been fun.' He wouldn't have given this up for anything. Not even to try his hand at snowboarding.

'But this might be the moment to let you know that overnight accommodation and a day on the ski slopes tomorrow is an option open to us. I had Housekeeping back at the hotel pack you an overnight case.'

He stared at her. She had? He moistened his lips. A whole day on the ski slopes.

'I didn't know what your timetable was like.' She shrugged. 'And I didn't want to pressure you, but...'

A grin built inside him. 'No, Addie, that is most definitely an option we should avail ourselves of.'

'Yes?'

'Yes.'

'Woo-hoo!' She jumped as if she meant to punch the air, but her skates shot out from beneath her. He grabbed her, yanking her back towards him and she landed against his chest, gripping his arms tightly when he wobbled too.

It brought her face in close and as their eyes met the laughter died on their lips. An ache swelled in his chest, his groin throbbed and he could barely breathe with the need to taste her.

Her gaze lowered to his lips and an answering hunger stretched through her face when she lifted her gaze back to his.

Once. Just once, he had to taste her.

His hands moved from her waist to her shoulders. Gripping them, he half lifted her as his lips slammed down to hers. Heat, sweetness and softness threatened to overwhelm him. She tasted like wine and cinnamon and her lips opened up at the sweep of his tongue as if she'd been yearning for his touch and had no interest in pretending otherwise.

Heat fireballed in his groin. Desire surged along

his veins and his lungs cramped. It was too much. He couldn't breathe. He let her go and took a step back feeling branded…feeling naked.

They stared at each other, both breathing hard, both clutching the railing with one hand for balance. And then she reached forward with her free hand, grabbed the lapels of his jacket and stretched up to slam her lips to his.

It knocked the breath out of him.

She explored every inch of his lips with minute precision, thoroughly and with relish. He wanted to moan, he wanted to grab her and…and make her his!

Her tongue dared his to dance. He answered the dare and took the lead, but she matched him kiss for kiss, her fire and heat rivals for his. They kissed until they had no breath left and then she let him go and stepped back. 'I…I've been wondering what it'd be like, kissing you.'

Sensational! 'Satisfied?'

'Uh huh.' She nodded. 'Oh, yes.'

Kisses like that, though, could open a whole can of worms and—

He jolted back when she touched his face. 'Christmas kisses don't count, Flynn.'

They didn't? Her eyes told him there'd be no more Christmas kisses, though.

Good thing. He bit back a sigh.

'Race you across to the other side.'

She set off. He set off after her. Afterwards he couldn't remember who had won.

They returned to Munich on Boxing Day evening, after a day of skiing and snowboarding. Flynn had even contemplated staying for another night and day. Addie had wanted to jump up and down and shout, 'Yes!'

But then she'd wondered if either of them would have the strength to resist another night of sitting by a log fire, the winter warmth and holiday freedom and the lure of following it through to its natural conclusion.

She figured Flynn must've had the same thought. And the same fear. She knew now, in a way she hadn't on that night when she'd propositioned him, that if they made love now her heart would be in danger and Flynn had made it plain where he stood on the relationship front. She had to respect that.

Even if he was being a great, big, fat, wrong-headed fool about it.

'What are you frowning at?' Flynn demanded as the elevator whooshed them up to the fourth floor.

'Oh…uh, just tired.'

'I don't believe you.'

He was too in tune with her. She scratched her neck. 'I was thinking about Frank and Jeannie.'

'Problem?'

'Not really, but would you mind if they stayed at the farmhouse with me for a while when I get back?'

'Why?'

'They're having trouble finding the right retirement village.'

'What would they do on the farm?'

Do? She frowned at him. 'Nothing.'

'Then why…?'

He let the sentence hang. 'The why is because they're my friends.' She wanted to thump him. 'The benefits are that Jeannie's a great cook and Frank has a wealth of knowledge and experience I could call on if it's needed.'

The elevator door opened and Flynn stepped out. 'You have more experience at breeding techniques than anyone else in the district.'

'And Frank has more when it comes to pasture

management, crop rotation and weed and pest control,' she said, keeping step beside him.

'I'd hazard a guess that Howard knows just as much about those subjects.'

'In Queensland Channel country maybe, but not in Mudgee.' She glared at him. 'Why is this an issue? It's not like they wouldn't be paying their own way.'

'It's an issue because I'm not running a retirement village at Lorna Lee's, Addie.'

She dropped her bag by her room door, folded her arms and widened her stance. 'We've talked about karma before, Flynn.'

'Yeah, and I'd better watch out, right?' He started to turn away.

'At Lorna Lee's we look after our own—whether they be human, animal or the land.'

He blew out a breath and turned back. 'How long would they stay?'

What was it to him? It was *her* house. 'A few months.' Maybe more. This should be up to her.

But it's not your house. Not any more. She swallowed.

'Okay, fine, yes. They can stay.' He glared at her. 'Happy?'

It occurred to her then that the answer to that might in fact be, No. She swallowed. 'Thank you.'

He slammed his hands to his hips. 'I was going to suggest that Room Service send up a plate of sandwiches and some hot chocolate, if you wanted to join me.'

An ache stretched through her chest. Did she dare?

'I still have your Christmas present in my case.'

That decided it. 'Give me half an hour to change and freshen up?'

With a nod he turned away.

Addie tripped into her room, a smile spreading through her. Had Flynn bought her something more than a dried plum and almond chimney sweep and a pair of mittens? Over the course of the last two days there hadn't been a suitable time to exchange their gifts. They'd done their best not to spend too much time on their own—especially after that kiss. They might not have actively sought out the company of others, but they'd tried to keep all of their exchanges public.

That kiss had happened in public.

Thanks heavens! Imagine where it would've led if they'd been somewhere private...intimate.

Like Flynn's room.

She shook that thought off. His bedroom in the suite next door was private—the door always firmly shut—but the rest of the suite was like the living room of a house. They'd be fine. As long as she remembered that she wanted to keep her heart intact and Flynn remembered he didn't sleep with his employees.

You don't have to be an employee. You wouldn't be an employee if...

She cut that thought dead and headed for the shower.

The phone rang as she pulled on a clean pair of jeans and a soft cashmere sweater in olive green that she'd bought on her shopping spree. Flynn had complimented her on it the first time she'd worn it. Which probably meant she should take it off.

She left it on and answered the phone.

'Fräulein Ramsey, it's Reception. There's a Herr Mueller to see you.'

What? She swallowed. 'I'll...' Um. 'I'll be right down.'

She led Herr Mueller into a small sitting room off to one side of Reception. She turned, gripping her hands together. 'I don't feel comfortable meeting you like this behind Flynn's back.'

'That does you credit, my dear, and I promise not to take up too much of your time.'

She sat and gestured for him to do the same. 'How can I help you?'

'I am very sorry—heartsick—at what Flynn experienced as a boy.'

That made the both of them.

'I did not know that Reuben, Flynn's father, would become so desperate as to take his own life. I hold myself partly responsible for that.'

Her stomach churned.

'I felt so let down and angry with him, and I let it blind me. I shouldn't have turned away from him so completely. It's not how friendship works.'

Her heart went out to the older man with his sad eyes and drooping shoulders. 'Herr Mueller, I don't believe you should take on that level of responsibility. I don't think anyone should.'

'Perhaps. Perhaps not. I do, however, understand Flynn's bitterness.'

She had no intention of talking about Flynn when he wasn't present.

'I understand it, but I will not let him take away everything for which my family has worked so hard.'

Flynn had made up his mind. She didn't see how Herr Mueller could stop him.

'Flynn is right. Reuben wasn't a thief—it wasn't he who stole the money.'

Her head shot up.

'It was his mistress—a barmaid at the pub called Rosie. Flynn and his mother never knew about her and I was grateful for that.' He sighed heavily. 'I'm afraid she had a cocaine habit that had spiralled out of control. Reuben covered up her misappropriation of funds as much as he could, but...' He shook his head. 'It couldn't go on and I'm afraid that when the money dried up she dumped him for someone younger and richer.'

She pressed a hand to her stomach. 'Why are you telling me this?'

He pulled a packet from his pocket. 'These are letters I found in Rosie's room after she left. They're the letters she and Reuben wrote to each other. There are also photographs. Some of them are quite...'

She winced and nodded.

'I didn't want either Flynn or his mother finding them.'

No.

'But it's obvious Flynn needs to see them now, needs to know the truth.'

She leapt to her feet. 'Oh, but—'

'The only question that remains—' he rose too '—is if this would come better from me or from you?'

Couldn't he see he was putting her in an impossible situation?

But when he held the packet out to her she took it, and then she turned and walked away without another word.

When she reached her room she sat on her bed. What to do? The moment she gave these letters and photographs to Flynn there'd be fireworks.

Big time.

Why couldn't Herr Mueller have just left them alone to have a nice Christmas?

She glanced at the presents she'd selected for Flynn, sitting on the coffee table waiting for her to take them across next door. She straightened. It was Boxing Day—a holiday and practically still Christmas. She wasn't going to let the past ruin today. Flynn hadn't had a proper Christmas in over twenty years.

She flung the packet into her bedside drawer. There'd be enough time for that tomorrow. Today was for presents and fun and relaxation. She collected up the presents and headed next door.

When Flynn opened his door at her knock, she had to reach right down into the depths of herself to find a smile. His lips twitched. 'You look beat.'

She seized hold of the excuse. 'The last time I was this bushed was when I went on muster when I was eighteen.'

'You went on a muster? But Lorna Lee's doesn't…'

'Oh, no.' She set his presents down, curled up into a corner of his sofa and helped herself to one of the tiny sandwiches on a platter sitting on the coffee table. 'It was on a station an hour north-west of us. A paying gig.' She shrugged. 'I wanted the experience.'

He folded himself into the armchair. 'Did you enjoy it?'

'Loved it.'

He stared at her. She shifted slightly. 'Would you be interested in mustering at my station every now and again just for the hell of it?'

Hell, yeah! Except… 'I…'

'Think about it.'

Right.

He rose. 'I ordered a pot of hot chocolate, but I'm going to have a beer.'

'Yes, please.'

After he was seated again a ripple of excitement fizzed through her. 'Present time!'

He laughed. 'You're like a big kid.'

'My father and I had a tradition of three presents. The first was something yummy, the second was something funny and the third was the real present.'

He glanced at the table where she'd lined up his presents, then at her, and his grin widened. He reached down beside his chair. 'One.' He lifted a brightly wrapped gift. 'Two.' A second one appeared. 'And three.'

She clapped her hands and beamed at him. 'My father would've liked you.'

They opened their first gifts—identical dried plum and almond chimney sweeps, of course.

Her second gift was a pair of woollen mittens— red and green with a print of fat white snowflakes sprinkled across them. Flynn grinned. 'They reminded me of the look on your face when you first saw it snowing.'

She clasped them to her chest. 'They're the best!' She'd treasure them.

'I'm almost frightened to open this,' he said when she handed him his second gift.

'I promise it doesn't bite.'

He tore open the wrapping to reveal a pair of lederhosen. He groaned and she laughed. 'I couldn't resist. Now it's your turn to go first.' She handed him his final present.

He tore off the wrapping paper and then just stared. She squirmed on her seat. She'd bought him a silver fountain pen. By chance when she'd been out walking one day she'd ambled into a quirky little shop that had specialised in all sorts of pens, including fountain pens. 'Do you like it?'

He pulled it free from his case. 'Addie, it's perfect. I'm not sure I've ever owned an object quite so beautiful.'

'I figure that given all the big contracts you sign that you ought to have a pen worthy of them.' She waved a finger at him. 'Now you have to promise to use it. You're not to put it away in some drawer to keep for good.'

He grinned. 'I promise. Now, here.' He handed her the final present.

She tried to open the paper delicately but in the end impatience overcame her and she simply tore it. Her jaw dropped. 'Oh!'

He leaned towards her. 'Do you like it?'

'No.' She shook her head. 'I *love* it!' He'd bought her a cuckoo clock—a marvellous and wonderful cuckoo clock. The local souvenir shops stocked them and they constantly fascinated her. Now she had one of her very own. 'Thank you!' She looked up. 'It's the best present ever.'

He grinned and he suddenly looked younger than she'd ever seen him. 'I wanted to give you a piece of Munich you'd be able to take home with you.'

Home...

She ran a finger across the little wooden frame of the cuckoo bird's house. 'You invited me along with you to Munich so I'd learn to really appreciate the things I have at home, didn't you?'

He shrugged and settled back in his chair. 'I hoped it would do that at the same time as ease your wanderlust.'

'It worked.'

'I'm glad.'

What he didn't know was that it had worked a little too well. She opened her mouth. She shook herself and shut it again. Tomorrow. There'd be time enough for all of that tomorrow.

She leaned forward and clinked her beer to his. 'Merry Christmas, Flynn. This has been a marvellous Christmas. Much better than expected. I'll never forget it.'

'I'll agree with each and every one of those statements. Merry Christmas, Addie.'

Addie drank in his smile and her heart twisted in her chest. It might, in fact, be the very last smile he ever gave her.

CHAPTER TEN

THE PULSE IN Addie's throat pounded when Flynn answered her knock on his door the next morning. She had to fight the urge to throw her arms around him and beg him not to hate her.

His gaze travelled down the length of her and his smile widened. 'I like your suits, Addie. I like them a lot, but I want you to know it's not necessary for you to don them every morning before you head on over here. I'll let you know in advance if we have a meeting.'

The pulse in her throat pounded harder. *Oh! Don't look at me like that.* As if he liked what he saw, as if she were a nice person. He wouldn't think her nice in a moment.

She gulped and moved into the suite on unsteady knees, setting the coffee pot onto the dining table as usual. She decided then that she hated her suits. She might burn them when she got home.

He frowned as if picking up on her mood. 'Is everything okay?'

She wiped her hands down her skirt and turned to face him. 'Not really.'

In two strides he was in front of her. 'Is everyone at Lorna Lee's okay? Jeannie and Frank? Bruce Augustus?'

His questions and the sincerity of his concern made her heart burn all the harder, made her love him all the more.

She straightened and blinked. Love? She swallowed. She didn't love him. She *liked* him a lot, but love?

He touched her arm. 'Addie?'

She moved out of his reach. 'It's nothing like that. As far as I know, everyone at home is fighting fit.'

She glanced at him. Had she fallen in love with Flynn? If so, did that change the things she needed to tell him?

She thought hard for a moment before shaking her head. She had to remember he didn't want her love—had warned her on that head more than once. Telling him she loved him would be his worst nightmare. She had no intention of making this interview harder for him than it'd already be.

She pushed her shoulders back. 'There are two things I need to tell you and you're not going to like either one of them. In fact, you're going to hate them.'

He stared at her. His brow lowered over his eyes and he folded his arms. 'Are you scared of me? Is that what this is about? You're scared I'm going to rant and rave and—'

'No.' She wheeled away to collect mugs, slammed them to the table. 'I mean, you'll probably rant and rave, but that doesn't scare me. It's just...'

He raised an eyebrow.

She bit back a sigh. 'It's just that you don't deserve it and I hate being the messenger.'

She pulled out a chair and fell into it. Flynn sat too, much more slowly and far more deliberately. 'You've been in contact with George Mueller.'

'He's been in contact with me,' she corrected, stung by the suspicion that laced his words.

'When?'

'Yesterday evening. I received a call from Reception that he was down there and wanted to see me.'

His face darkened. He leaned away from her, but his gaze didn't leave her face. 'Was that before or after our little supper?'

She swallowed. 'Before.' Her voice came out small.

The lines around his mouth turned white. 'And

what right did you think you had to withhold that piece of information from me?'

His voice emerged low and cold. She sensed the betrayal beneath his words and she wanted to drop her head to the table. 'I never had any intention of withholding the information from you. I just decided to delay it.'

'You had no right.'

'You don't even know what Herr Mueller spoke to me about yet.' She moistened her lips. 'Last night I hadn't worked out what I was going to do, so I made a judgment call. You obviously think it a bad one, but it's done now. In future it's probably a good idea to choose your PAs with more care, because I feel as if I'm in way over my head here, Flynn.'

He leapt out of his chair and wheeled away. 'You know how important closing this deal is to me. I can't believe you'd deliberately hold back something important and jeopardise negotiations.'

She stood, shaking. 'You don't even know yet what it was that Herr Mueller and I discussed, but you immediately leap to the worst possible conclusions. Can't you see how your obsession with this has clouded your judgment?'

He spun back. 'Clouded?' he spat.

'Yes!' she hollered at him. 'You've made it clear on more than one occasion how important this vendetta is to you.' So important he'd rather chase after it than live his life, enjoy his life.

He took his seat again. 'Sit,' he ordered, his voice containing not an ounce of compromise.

She sat.

'And now you will tell me everything.'

Her stomach churned. Her mouth went dry. She had to clear her throat before she could speak. 'Herr Mueller told me you were right—that your father didn't steal the money.'

A grim smile lit his lips. One hand clenched. 'I'm going to crush him like a bug.'

She closed her eyes. 'There is no easy way for me to tell you what he said next.' She opened them again. 'He said the thief was a barmaid called Rosie. He said that Rosie was your father's mistress.'

Flynn shot out of his chair so quickly it crashed to the floor. It barely made a sound against the thick carpet. He stabbed a finger at Addie. 'That is a dirty, filthy lie.'

Addie folded her arms. For the first time he noted her pallor and the dark circles beneath her eyes.

'Was your father really such a paragon of perfection?' she whispered.

'He wasn't a thief and he wasn't a cheat!'

'Even if he had been both of those things, it doesn't mean he wasn't a good father.'

What on earth was she talking about?

She stared at him, her amber eyes alternately flashing and clouding. 'You love him so much that I think he must've been a wonderful father, but you did say what a difficult woman your mother always was. Would it really be such a stretch to believe that he found comfort elsewhere?'

It went against everything Flynn believed in.

'This is the version of events Herr Mueller relayed to me. I don't know if they're lies or not. I'm just telling you what he said.'

He righted his chair and sat, nodded once in a way that he hoped hid the ache that stretched through his chest. She glanced at the coffee pot and he leaned forward and poured her a mug.

She curled her hands around it. 'Thank you.'

This situation wasn't of her making. He knew how much she hated it. She'd never pretended otherwise. But she'd no right to hold this back from him. 'Go on.' His voice came out harder and curter than he'd meant it to. When, really, all he wanted to do was reach out and take her hand and tell her how sorry he was that he'd dragged her into his sordid game. She must be wishing herself a million miles away. He dragged a hand down his face.

'He said Rosie had a cocaine problem. She stole money from the pub—lots of it—and when he realised your father tried to cover it up. Of course, the money dried up at that point and Rosie apparently dumped him for someone younger and richer.' She pulled in a breath. 'Herr Mueller said he felt betrayed by your father and turned his back on him. He says he regrets that now and wishes he'd done things differently.'

This was all a fantasy, a fiction. 'And you believed him?'

Addie met his gaze. 'I don't think it matters what I believe. It's what you believe that's important.'

Had she and George been in this together from the start? Had George promised her that she could see the world if she came and worked for him?

She reached down into her briefcase and pulled out a package. 'He gave these to me. He says they're letters your father and Rosie wrote to each other. And photographs. I haven't looked at them. They're none of my business.' She set them on the table. 'I can't help feeling they're none of yours either.'

His head snapped up. She grimaced and shrugged. 'Mind you, you're talking to the woman who wouldn't read the letters her parents left behind when they...' She trailed off with another shrug.

Flynn seized the package and waved it at her. 'Letters can be forged. Photographs can be doctored.'

She swallowed. 'True.' But he could see that in this instance she didn't believe they had been.

'What else did he say?'

She nodded at the package. 'He said he took those so you and your mother wouldn't find them, wouldn't find out about Rosie. And...' she pulled in a breath '...he wanted to know if I thought this news would come better from him or from me.'

'So you made another judgment call?'

She glanced down at her hands. 'I'm sorry if I made the wrong one.'

Was she?

She straightened. Her pallor tugged at him. 'Flynn, you have your father on a pedestal—an impossibly high one. I'm not even sure if you're aware of that. Why? Is it because the last time you truly felt safe was when your father was alive? I understand about honouring the dead, but—'

'Oh, yes, you know all about that, don't you?' He wheeled on her, wanting—needing—her to stop. 'Honouring the dead, putting them on pedestals! Look at what you've done to Robbie.'

She stood too. 'Yes, I did put her on a pedestal. I didn't know how else to deal with my grief, but you showed me how doing so had narrowed my view. You helped me realise I was in danger of making a big mistake. I'm working on it, trying to put it into some kind of perspective and make it better. And you have to learn to do the same.' She lifted her arms. 'Is this really what your father would want from you?'

His scalp crawled. 'Don't you presume to tell me what my father would want from me. You didn't know him and you don't know George Mueller!'

Her eyes flashed and she strode forward to poke him in the chest. 'What happens to us when we're young can leave scars—big, ugly, jagged ones. But I'm here to tell you that you're a grown man now—a grown man with the backing of a powerful financial empire you've built yourself. Nobody and nothing can take your achievements away from you. It's time to recognise that fact. It's time you stopped chasing demons and trying to slay imaginary dragons. It's time you started acting like a man!'

All he could do was stare at her.

'If your father was the paragon of perfection that you claim, then so be it. But paragons don't kill themselves, Flynn. In which case he wasn't perfect. In which case deal with it and move on.'

He wanted to smash something. He wanted to run away. He wanted—

He strode away from her towards the window, dragging both hands back through his hair. The street below had become alive with cars and people.

If Herr Mueller wasn't guilty...

He shook that thought off. Of course he was guilty! This was just his latest attempt to save his neck. He opened the window to let in a blast of icy air, but it did nothing to clear the confusion rolling through him.

He might be a grown man, but the terror and confusion when he'd learned of his father's death still felt as raw and real to him now as it had when he'd been twelve years old. He gripped the window frame so hard the wood bit into his hand. He'd tried to bury that scared little boy when he'd made his first million. It hadn't worked. He didn't doubt for a moment, though, that taking George Mueller down would quieten the demons that plagued him.

'The ball is now in your court,' Addie said. 'What happens now is up to you.'

He knew that if it were up to her she'd have him walk away. Well, it wasn't up to her. He slammed the window shut and spun around, cloaking the war raging inside him behind an icy wall. 'You said you had two things to tell me. What's the second thing?'

Her gaze slid away. 'You know what?' She seized her briefcase. 'I think you should consider what Herr Mueller had to say and we can discuss the other issue tomorrow. I—'

'Don't presume to tell me what I should do.'

She dropped her briefcase back to the floor, pushed her shoulders back and met his gaze squarely. 'You're no more a lackey than I am, so maybe you'll understand what I'm about to say… and do.'

Something inside him froze. He didn't know why but he wanted to beg her to stop. He wanted it to start snowing and for her face to light up as she dashed out into it. 'What do you mean to do?' he said instead. He'd have winced at the sheer hard brilliance of his voice, but he couldn't. It was as if an invisible barrier stood between him and the rest of the world.

She twisted her hands together. 'I'm not going to sell you Lorna Lee's, Flynn. I'm going to take advantage of the cooling-off period stated in our contract and renege on our deal.'

Her words knocked the breath out of him. It took all of his strength not to stagger. The dream of a home of his own, a place where he could belong and be himself, slipped out of reach, evaporated into a poof of nothingness.

They'd just spent two amazing days in the Alps and all that time she'd been planning to pull out of their deal?

'You were right. I'm not lackey material.' Her hands continued to twist. 'The more I consider having to take orders from anyone in relation to Lorna Lee's, the more everything inside me rebels. It's my home.' She slapped a hand to her chest. 'I want to be the one who shapes it, to determine which direction it should take...and to decide who can and can't live there.'

Apparently she didn't want *him* living there.

He folded his arms, something inside him hardening. 'You're doing this because you don't approve of my business dealings with Mueller. If you think this will turn me back from that course of action, you're sadly mistaken.'

'To hell with Herr Mueller,' she shot back rudely. 'And to hell with you too, Flynn. I'm doing this for me!' Her hands clenched. 'Did you really not see this coming? As far as I can tell you've been one step ahead of me when it comes to my true feelings.' She moved in closer to peer up into his face. 'I want to be the one to call the shots. I don't want to be told to get rid of a beloved bull or that I can't have Frank and Jeannie live with me. I don't want to be your lackey, Flynn, and I don't want to be Robbie's either. I just…I just want to be my own person.'

'Pretty speech,' he taunted, 'but what about your neighbours? They need this sale.'

'The bank will lend me the money to buy them out.'

He could feel his face twist. 'You've checked already?'

'Oh, for heaven's sake, are you really that intent on seeing conspiracies all around you? I checked with the bank before you ever made on offer on the place in case it became the only option.'

'I could fight you on this.'

'What?' It was her turn to taunt. 'Are you going to turn me into your next vendetta? Are you going to do everything in your power to destroy me?'

Of course not, but…

'The funny thing is it's you who's responsible for my change of heart. You dared me to discover what it was I really wanted. And Lorna Lee's is what I really want.' She threw her arms up and wheeled away. 'Yes, I also want to travel and see the world, but I want a home base. I want to live in the world where I grew up, where Robbie grew up and where all of my friends are. I want to work at something I'm good at and I want to canter over green fields at the end of a day's honest work and to know I'm where I should be.' She bit her lip and glanced up at him. 'Maybe that's the way you feel about your property in Channel country.'

He didn't feel that way about anywhere. He'd thought he might find it at Lorna Lee's but… He cut off that thought. He had no intention of sharing it with her.

'There'll be no cash injection for expansion.'

Something in her eyes told him he'd disappointed her. 'I'm well aware of that. Expansion is something I can work towards.'

So that was that, then, was it?

She swiped her hands down the front of her skirt. 'I want to thank you, Flynn. I suspect it's no comfort, but you've helped me—'

'Spare me!'

She flinched.

'I should've known you were trouble the moment I heard you bawling to that darn bull.'

Her intake of breath told him he'd hit the mark. Finally.

She brushed a hand across her eyes. 'You heard that?'

He kinked an eyebrow because a ball of stone had lodged in his chest, making it impossible to speak.

Her eyes shimmered. She swallowed hard. 'You offered me Munich because you felt sorry for me?' She stared at him as if she'd never seen him before. 'I don't get you at all.'

He forced a harsh laugh. 'But you did, didn't you? You've taken me for a complete ride. You weaselled a free trip to Munich out of me, sabotaged my business dealings while we were here and then reneged on a contract I'd signed in good faith. You must be laughing up your sleeve.'

She paled. 'That's not true.'

He shrugged and turned away as if he didn't care, as if none of it mattered to him. 'I think it'd be best all round if you just caught the first available flight back to Australia, don't you?'

'I know you're angry with me at the moment and disappointed about Lorna Lee's, but we're friends! I'm sorry, truly sorry, that things have turned out this way. If there's anything I can do to make amends...I mean, I'm still your PA for as long as you need me to and—'

'Don't bother. I'll hire someone competent.'

That was hardly fair, but he didn't care. He wanted Addie and all of her false promises gone. He didn't need reminding how bad his judgment was when it came to women. 'Like I said, it's time you were out of my hair.'

Silence and then, 'If that's what you want.'

He kept his back to her even though something in her voice chafed at him. 'That's exactly what I want.' His heart bellowed a protest, but he ignored it.

The click of the door told him that she was gone. For good.

He limped over to the armchair and sank into it, closing his eyes and trying to shut his mind to the pain that flooded him.

Addie stumbled back into her room. She glanced from side to side, turned on the spot and then kicked herself forward to perch on the sofa. She clutched a cushion to her stomach.

Oh, that hadn't gone well.

It was never going to go well.

Perhaps not, but she hadn't realised it would leave her feeling so depleted. So guilty. So hurt.

She dropped to her knees on the floor and pressed her face into the soft leather of the sofa. There had to be something she could do to make things right between them. It was such poor form to back out of the Lorna Lee sale. He'd made his offer fair and square, he'd gone to the expense of bringing a foreman in, he'd brought her to Munich, but…

Lorna Lee's was her home. It was where she belonged. Surely Flynn could understand that. Surely—

Everything inside her froze. She uncurled herself from the floor to stand. He didn't, though, did he? She moved to the window, but the view outside didn't register. Flynn bought things—he owned them, developed them and once he'd done that he sold them off at a profit—but he had no roots. There wasn't a single place he called home. Lorna Lee's wouldn't have been any different— just another in a long line of enterprises. Flynn shunned those kind of roots while she, she'd discovered, craved them.

'So, why so heartbroken?' she whispered into the silence.

Because none of it stops you from loving him.

For a moment she was too tired even for tears. She just stood there and stared out at a grey sky.

Flynn sat in his room. He sat and did nothing. He tried to feel nothing. Addie's news had shattered something inside him.

Not her revelation of Herr Mueller's spurious allegations. He hadn't expected any less from the other man. That had angered him, true, but it occurred to him now that much of his anger was directed at himself—for creating a situation where Addie had been forced to play go-between, that he'd involved her in dealings that turned her stomach.

Revenge might be satisfying, but it wasn't noble. He should've kept her well away from it. He glanced at the packet of letters and photographs. *Not your business.* He seized them, stalked into the bedroom and threw them into the bottom of his suitcase, threw the suitcase to the top of the wardrobe and stalked back into the living area. He threw himself back into his chair.

It wasn't Mueller's machinations that maddened

him—he'd been expecting those. It was Addie's news that she wasn't going to sell him Lorna Lee's.

He leapt up and paced from one side of the room to the other. He flung out an arm. Contract-wise she was well within her rights to pull out. Besides, it wasn't as if he wouldn't be able to purchase another cattle property just like Lorna Lee's. So why did he feel so betrayed?

Because he'd thought them friends?

He dragged a hand down his face. This was business. It wasn't personal. It had nothing to do with friendship. She hadn't pulled out with the intention of hurting him.

He bent to rest his hands on his knees and dragged in a breath. He could buy another farm, but he wouldn't have Addie working for him. It wouldn't be a place that eased his soul when he entered its gates. It wouldn't feel like home.

He stumbled back to his chair.

Addie pulling out of their deal had shattered a dream he'd hardly realised had been growing within him. He would now never get the chance to work with her—to experience and observe her expertise, to witness her excitement when he gave her the opportunity to expand her programme. He would never get the chance to laugh with her, discuss moral issues, travel with her and…and experience the world through her eyes. A more attractive world than the one in which he lived.

That's your choice.

He shot upright. What the hell? He'd started to do what he'd sworn he'd never do again—become involved with a woman. His hands clenched. In walking away, Addie had done them both a favour. His realisation at the near miss had him resting his hands on the back of a chair and breathing deeply. He wasn't giving another woman the opportunity to stomp all over his heart. Not even Addie.

He didn't doubt she'd do her best to treat his heart with care and kindness, but eventually he'd make some mistake, do something wrong, and she'd turn away.

He swallowed, fighting the vice-like pain gripping his chest. When he could move again he pulled on a tracksuit and running shoes and headed outside. He ran by the Isar, drawing the scent of the river and winter into his lungs. His world might never become as congenial and gratifying as Addie's, but he wouldn't forget to appreciate the little things again.

Your world will never be like hers for as long as you continue with your vendetta.

He shook that thought off. Herr Mueller deserved everything that was coming to him.

He ran and ran until he was sick of sliding on the ice-slicked paths, and then he walked. He walked for miles and miles. He walked until he was exhausted and then he turned and headed back to the hotel—miles away.

Flynn had just passed beneath the Isartor in all of its medieval grandness when Addie emerged from the hotel doors with Bruno at her side carrying her bags. The concierge had obviously chosen to wait on Addie himself rather than leave it to a porter. They moved towards a waiting taxi. Flynn's heart started to pound. He stepped back beneath the tor, into the shadows where Addie wouldn't see him.

You could stop this.

All he'd have to do was call out...ask her to stay. Would she?

He recalled the way she'd looked at him earlier, the way her voice had trembled, and knew she would. He closed his eyes and rested his head back against aged stone. Addie might be willing to risk her heart, but he wasn't.

He remained in the shadows until the taxi had driven away. He leant against the wall and pretended to study the structure like the other sightseers until he had the strength to push forward. He didn't want to go back to the hotel, but…

There was nowhere else to go.

Bruno greeted him as he entered. 'Good afternoon, Herr Mather.' He didn't smile.

Was it afternoon already?

'Miss Addie got away safely for her flight home.'

He swallowed. 'Excellent.'

'She asked me to give you this.'

He handed Flynn the carved bull—Bruce Augustus—and a letter.

Dammit! He'd given her that bull as a gift.

At the last moment he remembered his manners—it was almost as if Addie had dug him in the ribs. 'Thank you, Bruno.'

He moved towards the elevator. He should wait until he was in his room, but… He tore the letter open.

Dear Flynn,
You gave me this as a promise, but as I broke mine to you I don't feel I have the right to keep it.

He clenched his hand so hard the carving dug into it.

I'm sorry I disappointed you and let you down. My life is better for knowing you, but I understand that you can't say the same.

A lump weighed in his chest. His eyes burned.

I don't want you to think I took advantage of you on purpose. Please send me the bill for my share of the trip to Munich. Don't worry. I do have the funds to cover it.

Not a chance!

From the bottom of my heart—thank you. For everything. If you ever find yourself in the neighbourhood drop in for a cuppa. You can always be assured of a warm welcome at Lorna Lee's.

He wanted to accept that invitation. Everything inside him clamoured for him to.

Love, Addie.

He folded the letter. He wanted it too badly. It was why he had to resist.

'Flynn, I'm glad I caught you.'

He stiffened. George Mueller.

A fist tightened about his chest and did all it

could to squeeze the air from his body. 'Herr Mueller, I'm afraid I'm not in the mood at the moment.' He turned. 'And don't bother pestering Adelaide again. She's no longer here.' He pushed the button for the elevator.

George scanned his face and something inside him seemed to sag. 'You sent her away.'

He didn't reply to that.

The older man shook his head. 'You still refuse to see the truth.'

'The one truth I do know is that whatever happened between my father and you, you turned away from him. You turned away from my mother and you turned away from me. You call that friendship? I don't think so. If nothing else, that defines you, indicates the kind of man you are.'

The elevator door slid open. Flynn stepped inside and pushed the button for the fourth floor.

Mueller reached out a hand to stop it closing. 'It is the greatest regret of my life, Flynn. I'm sorry. I should've tried harder, but when I contacted your mother she wanted nothing to do with me. I thought…'

Mueller had contacted his mother?

'I understand it's easier to hate me. Maybe I do deserve all of this, but I can't believe you sent that lovely girl away when anyone could see how much she cared for you.'

If Addie did care for him, she'd get over it. It was better this way.

Mueller straightened and met Flynn's gaze squarely. 'You can take away my business and my livelihood, you can ruin me financially, but you can never take from me my family. You will never be able to turn my loved ones against me because they love me as strongly as I love them. And for all your money and your power, Flynn, I can't help thinking that still makes me the richer man.'

Nausea churned in the pit of his stomach.

'Where is that love and connection in your life, I ask myself? You're so intent on the past that you have no future. Regardless of what you do, I would not trade places with you.'

Mueller shook his head, real disgust reflected in his eyes. 'You sent her away. You're a fool. Careful, Flynn, or you'll find yourself in danger of becoming the cruel, heartless man you think I am.'

And then he moved and the elevator door slid closed.

On the flight home, Addie fired up her laptop and opened her 'Till the Cows Come Home' diary.

Dear Daisy
What I wouldn't give to see you right now. I need a smile and a shoulder.

In her mind's eye she conjured that exact smile and the precise dimensions of Robbie's shoulders. How had she thought she'd ever forget?

I've fallen in love. I've fallen in love with a man who thinks I don't possess a faithful bone in my body—a man who thinks I used him.

And then it all came tumbling out—the whole rush of falling in love with Flynn, of trying to resist him, of how his reasons for being in Munich had filled her with misgiving. She told Daisy how kind and thoughtful he was, how his zeal could capture hold of him and fire him to life and how that had always stolen her breath. She relayed how he dreamed impossible dreams and made them come true.

Daisy, I've fallen in love with a man I'm never going to see again and I don't know what to do.

What would she like to have happen?

I'd like for him to turn up next week at Lorna Lee's and tell me he loves me too; that he's pre-

pared to risk his heart one more time because he trusts me. That's what I want, but I know it's impossible.

She moistened her lips. She'd never had a chance to tell Flynn how she felt about him. There'd be no point in trying to contact him now. He'd refuse to take her calls, would delete her emails. He would never seek out her company or speak to her again. She didn't hold any hope that he'd ever return her feelings. He'd warned her. He'd told her he didn't do relationships.

She closed the lid of her laptop. She should've listened.

CHAPTER ELEVEN

TWO DAYS LATER Flynn snapped his laptop closed. It was pointless. There wasn't a scrap of dirt or scandal to be found on George Mueller. How could that be?

He glanced at the contract. Finally...*finally* it was his. All it required was his signature and George Mueller would be a ruined man.

He strode to the window. Correction—Mueller would be financially ruined. He wouldn't fall into the same pit of despair Flynn's father had. He wouldn't kill himself.

He snapped away, heart pounding. He didn't want the other man to kill himself! He dragged a hand down his face. He just wanted justice.

Addie's face rose up in his mind and raised an eyebrow.

He swung back to the window. Today the sky in Munich was blue and he could see the frosty air on the breath of the passers-by below.

Are you sure he's guilty?

He glanced at his watch, drummed his fingers on the window ledge before straightening and stalking over to the telephone. He punched in a number.

'Hello, Mum, it's Flynn,' he said when she answered.

'What do you want?'

Hello, son, lovely to hear from you. He bit back his sarcasm, but dispensed with pleasantries. 'I want to know if George Mueller ever contacted you after Dad died.'

A pause followed.

'And I want the truth.'

'Things are really tight around here at the moment...'

He glared at the ceiling. 'How much do you want?'

She named a sum.

'I'll have it wired into your account by the close of business today.'

She didn't even thank him.

'George Mueller?' he prompted.

'He paid for your father's funeral.'

Flynn sat, swallowed. 'Why?'

'It was the least he could do! We'd been happy before him and your father became partners in that cursed pub. Why do you want to know about him after all this time?'

Her strident tone scratched through him. 'Because our paths have crossed again. I'm in Munich and...' He trailed off.

There was another pause and then a harsh laugh. 'You're there to take over his company, aren't you?'

Yes.

'Do it!' she ordered. 'Let him see what it feels like to lose what he's worked so hard for. Let him see what it's like when the shoe is on the other foot.'

Bile burned the back of his throat. 'I have to go.'

'The money...you won't forget?'

'No,' he ground out. 'I won't forget.'

He slammed down the phone. Her bitterness and her antipathy made his stomach churn and his temples pound. He had an insane urge to shower, to wash the dirt off, but he'd only showered a few short hours ago. *Let him see what it feels like to lose what he's worked so hard for.* His hands clenched. She'd never worked hard a day in her life! Unless you counted her incessant nagging of his father.

He rested his head in his hands before lifting it with a harsh laugh. 'The apple doesn't fall far from the tree, does it?' Was this the man he'd truly become? He'd been so busy putting his father on a pedestal that he hadn't realised that all of this time he'd been turning into his mother.

He suddenly wished Addie were here to tell him he was wrong and that he was nothing like his mother.

He swallowed the bile that rose in his throat. Addie was where she belonged. And he... He finally had Mueller exactly where he wanted him. So why was he hesitating?

Flynn took a leaf from Addie's book and went sightseeing. He strode up to the Residenz and lost himself in art and architecture. He absorbed himself in accounts of history utterly foreign to him. Four hours later he found himself in the coffee shop above Marienplatz where he and Addie had once shared coffee.

He ordered coffee and apple strudel. He stared at the town halls—old and new—and wondered what on earth he was doing there. Sitting here without Addie cracked something open in his chest, something he wasn't sure he'd ever be able to shut again. He threw money onto the table and strode back out having barely touched his refreshments.

He stalked the streets, round and round, coming to an abrupt halt when he almost collided with a statue of three stone oxen. They lorded it over a fountain that tripped down levels like a gentle waterfall.

Oxen…cattle…Bruce Augustus…Addie.

He collapsed on a nearby bench to stare at the statue, recalling the way Addie had cried against the giant bull's shoulder. He'd bet it was the first thing she'd done when she'd returned to Lorna Lee's—headed straight down to the bull's pen.

He rested his head in his hands. And she'd have cried. His abrupt dismissal would've made her cry. For a moment he wished he had a Bruce Augustus too.

For heaven's sake. He lifted his head. He didn't want coffee and cake. He didn't want Bruce Augustus. He wanted Addie. What was the point in hiding from it?

Yeah, well, you can't have her.

His mouth filled with acid and his future with darkness. Who said? Maybe he—

You said.

He pulled in a breath and nodded. He'd said. And it was for the best. It'd be for the best all round if he just stopped thinking about her.

Ha! As if that were possible.

Do what you came here to do and then go home and put it all behind you.

He slumped back against the bench, staring at the oxen. Why was he hesitating?

Because once it was done it would put him out of Addie's reach forever.

He shot to his feet. She was out of reach already!

Flynn strode back to the hotel. He made sure to enquire after Bruno's mother's health—the older woman was ailing—and sped straight up to his room. He strode over to the contract, pulled the pen Addie had given him from its case and scrawled his signature along the bottom.

Done.

His stomach churned. The blood in his veins turned alternately hot and cold. If he'd been expecting peace he'd have been seriously disappointed.

If he went through with this, there would never be a chance for him and Addie. He dragged a hand down his face. If he didn't go through with it there were no guarantees that there'd ever be a chance for him and Addie either.

If he went through with this it'd prove he was exactly like his mother.

His mouth dried. His heart pounded. What would his father choose in the same situation?

Love. The answer came to him from some secret place filled with truth. His father would've chosen love. His father would've chosen Addie.

He fell into a seat, frozen. He'd sent Addie away. She hadn't wanted to go. A lump stretched his throat in a painful ache. He blinked against the burning in his eyes.

If only he dared, could she be his?

Did he dare?

The blood pounded so hard in his ears it deafened him. He stood, but he didn't know what to do so he sat again. *Think!* Make no mistake, Addie would want it all—marriage, kids, commitment. Did he dare risk it? Could he make a marriage with Addie work?

If it went wrong he wasn't sure he'd have the strength to dust himself off again.

He stared across the room and the longer he stared, the darker it seemed to get. A choice lay before him that would affect the rest of his life. It would define the very man he'd become.

He could choose his mother's way—bitterness and revenge.

Or he could choose Addie and love; but with no guarantees.

He strode over to the contract, seized it in his hands. He'd spent a lifetime working towards this. Addie would never have to know if...

But you'd know.

'Relax, Bruce Augustus.' Addie petted the giant bull's shoulder as she settled on the fence. 'I haven't come down here to cry all over you.'

She'd been home for ten whole days and she'd spent more of that time bawling all over her poor old pal than she had in deciding Lorna Lee's future. The secret crying had helped her keep up a semi-cheerful façade for everyone else, but it hadn't made the ache in her heart go away.

She forced herself to smile. Wasn't that supposed to make you feel better? She grimaced. If so, it was a lie.

No, no. She forced another smile. 'Today we have good news, Bruce Augustus. Today the bank agreed to lend me the money to buy out Frank and Jeannie and the Seymours.'

Jeannie and Frank were going to pay her a nominal rent on their house. She'd told them they could stay for as long as they wanted. Without the worry of having to work the land they'd developed a new lease of life. Addie was glad. She'd rent out the Seymour house too and it'd give her enough money to hire an additional hand. She'd had interest from several local farmers who wanted to agist their stock here if she were amenable. It'd all help pay the mortgage.

She turned to gaze out at the land that rolled away in front of her. Dams twinkled silver in the sunlight, grass rustled and bent in the breeze and the enormous and ancient gums stood as brooding and eternal as ever. She pressed a hand to her chest when she realised how closely she'd come to giving it all away.

'My home,' she whispered. She belonged here. It was where she wanted to be. But that didn't make the ache in her heart go away either.

She turned back to Bruce Augustus. 'I know you're sick of me talking about Flynn, but I worked something out. It's like emotionally I've been through a flood or a drought or a bushfire. Anyway—' she shook her head '—it doesn't matter what it is specifically, just that it's some kind of natural disaster. And it takes time to rebuild after something like that.'

Bruce Augustus remained silent.

'I know, I know.' She sighed. 'I have no idea how long it'll take either.'

She kicked the ground, picked a splinter of wood from the railing. She heard a car purr up the driveway. 'Sounds like we have company.' She peeked around the side of the pen when the car pulled to a halt outside the homestead. 'A black Mercedes Benz,' she told her bull, moving back into the privacy provided by the pen. 'There were lots of those in Munich. Funny thing I've noticed recently, but in the movies and on cop shows the villains always seem to drive a black Mercedes.'

She glanced back to see who would emerge from the car and then slammed back, flattening herself against the railing. Her heart hammered. Flynn! 'What's he doing here?' Had he come with his big guns to enforce the contract they'd signed?

She forced air into cramped lungs. 'Don't you worry, Bruce Augustus. I got legal advice about that.' He'd have a fight on his hands if he tried anything.

She pushed her shoulders back and moved towards the house, and slammed right into Flynn as he rounded the corner. 'Oh!'

He reached out to steady her. 'I thought I'd find you down here.'

She wanted to hurl herself into his arms. She

forced herself to step back. His arms dropped back to his sides. She made herself smile brightly. 'So, you were in the area and decided to pop in for a cuppa?'

Gently he shook his head. 'No.' And her heart sank.

'I see.'

He frowned. 'You do?'

She pushed her chin up. 'Flynn, you ought to know that I did get legal advice. I was well within my rights to pull out of the sale when I did.'

His frown deepened.

'You can drag me through the courts if you want to and it may take years to settle, but no court in the country will rule against me and in the end you'll be forced to pay all of the court costs and I won't be any the worse off. I know you're angry with me, but do you really think that's the best use of your time and money?'

He turned grey. 'Of course that's what you'd think of me.'

Her heart burned. She ached to pull his head down to her shoulder.

'I haven't come here to try and take your home from you, Addie.'

The breeze ruffled his hair. She stared at it, wanting—

'Addie?'

She started. 'You haven't?'

He shook his head.

Okay, that was good to know, but... 'How was Herr Mueller when you left Munich?'

'I don't know.' He wore a business suit and she wanted to tear it off him and force him into jeans and a T-shirt. 'I didn't see him, but I expect he's relieved. I burned the contract and left Munich.'

She gripped a post to stop from falling over. 'You did what?' It didn't make sense. 'You...you read the letters, saw the photos and...'

'No, I burned those too. Bruno and I had quite the blaze. He sends his best, by the way.'

She rubbed her forehead. 'What does Bruno have to do with it?'

'There weren't fireplaces in our rooms, see, but he let me light one in the guest lounge.'

She pressed a hand to her forehead and breathed in deeply. 'Let me get this straight. You burned the contract?'

'Yes.'

She straightened. 'You found out some other way that Herr Mueller wasn't a cheat and a thief?'

He shook his head, but his eyes burned into hers. 'I'm never going to know the truth of what happened back then. I very much doubt, though, that

George Mueller is the monster I made him out to be. The thing is, you were right about those letters. They weren't any of my business. They were written by two people who'd have been mortified to discover I'd ever read them. And once I understood that I realised the whole affair between Mueller and my father was none of my business either.'

She stared at him. 'Wow.'

'You were right on another head. Slaying that dragon wouldn't bring my father back. It wouldn't right wrongs and it wouldn't turn back time. It'd just start a whole new cycle of hate. I chose to turn my back and walk away.'

She couldn't get out a second wow. Her lungs had cramped too much.

As if he found it hard to meet her gaze, he turned to the bull. 'Hey, Bruce Augustus, how're you doing?'

The bull eyeballed him. Addie took his arm and edged him away. 'Old Bruce Augustus here can take a while to warm to strangers.'

She led them to a large boulder beneath an enormous spreading gum, and then gestured to his suit. 'You might get dirty. Would you like to go up to the house for a cold drink or…?'

His answer was to settle on the rock. After a moment's hesitation she settled down beside him.

'I wanted to come by and tell you that I harbour no hard feelings about you pulling out of the sale.'

She stared from her feet and up into the cool blue of his eyes. 'You mean that?'

'This is your home, Addie. You belong here. I'm glad you realised that. The cooling-off clause in a contract is there for a reason.'

A weight lifted from her. 'Thank you.'

'I also wanted to return this.' He pulled the carved bull from his pocket. 'I gave this to you last time to seal a verbal contract. I'm giving it to you this time as a token of gratitude.'

She took the miniature Bruce Augustus with a smile. 'I missed this. But, Flynn, I don't see what I could have possibly done to inspire gratitude.' That belonged solely to her, surely?

His eyes dimmed. 'You pulled me back from the brink. You stopped me from making a mistake and doing a very bad thing.'

He glanced at her with such a look in his eyes her heart started to hammer.

'You once warned me about karma. I don't want it to come calling on me to kick my butt.'

That made her grin. She forced her gaze away. In

the sky, miles away, a wedge-tail eagle circled on lazy drifts of warm air. She kept her gaze trained on it rather than the man beside her. She'd spent the last ten days crying over him and she was glad he'd taken the time to tell her all he had, but she needed him to go now. It was too hard seeing him and not being able to…

'Could we go for a gallop?'

She closed her eyes. 'Why?'

'Because I want to see that look of absolute contentment and relish on your face again. I missed it when you left Munich.'

'When you sent me away,' she corrected, turning to finally meet the gaze that burned through her.

'Guilty as charged.'

What did he want? 'I appreciate you taking time out of your busy schedule, Flynn, but you could've sent the carving through the mail. You could've explained everything else in an email. Why are you here?'

'I wanted to see you.'

'Why?'

She swallowed when she recognised the flare of hunger that crossed his face. Wow! She folded her arms to keep from reaching for him. 'I'm no longer an employee. That means…'

He folded his arms too and raised an eyebrow. 'What does it mean?'

Her heart sank. 'That I now tick your box as temporary girlfriend material.'

'There's nothing temporary about you, Addie.'

She let out a breath. 'I'm glad you realise that.' She knew in her bones that if she had an affair with Flynn her heart would never fully recover.

'Which is why I was going to ask you to marry me.'

She leapt off the rock as if scalded. 'I beg your pardon?'

His expression didn't change. 'You heard. You might have trouble taking orders, but there's nothing wrong with your hearing.'

'I...' *Say yes, you fool!* She thrust out her jaw. 'Why would I take a risk on someone with such a poor matrimonial record?'

One side of his mouth hooked up. 'Because you love me, perhaps?'

Her heart thumped. How did he know that? Was she so transparent?

'And because I love you.'

She stared at him. Her knees trembled. 'Why would you go and change your mind so completely about matrimony?'

He didn't answer. She glared. 'You must really want Lorna Lee's.'

He turned so grey and haggard she almost threw her arms around him. 'When you left Munich, Addie...when I so stupidly sent you away, your absence left such a hole inside me that I couldn't fill it up.'

She swallowed. She had to plant her feet to stop from swaying towards him.

'All I wanted was you, but I didn't believe I could have you. And then I spoke to my mother.'

What did his mother have to do with it? 'Your mother?' she prompted when he didn't continue.

He shook himself. 'She's so bitter. When she found out I was in Munich she ordered me to destroy Mueller.'

She tried to swallow the bad taste that rose in her mouth.

'That's when I realised I'd become just like her.'

Oh, no, he wasn't, he—

'And I don't want to be like her, Addie. I want to be like my father.' He swallowed, vulnerability stretching through his eyes. 'I want to be like you.'

He did?

'To be worthy of you, I knew I'd have to give up my vendetta and initially that was a struggle.' The lines framing his eyes and bracketing his mouth deepened for a moment. 'In the end, though, I wanted to choose the future instead of the past. I wanted to be a man who built a life he could be proud of. And, Addie...' his gaze speared hers '...I want that life with you. I love you.'

Golden light pierced her from the inside out. She tossed her head, her smile growing. 'Why haven't you kissed me yet?'

He closed the gap between them in an instant and pulled her into his arms. 'Because I'm afraid that once I start I won't be able to stop,' he growled.

'I wouldn't mind,' she whispered against his lips the moment before they claimed hers.

Her head rocked back from the force of the kiss, but his hand moved to her nape to steady her. 'Sorry.' He lifted his head. 'I—'

She dragged his head back down to hers and kissed him back with the same ferocity. Her arms wrapped around him. His arms wrapped around her and they kissed and kissed. His kisses told her of his struggles and how much he'd missed her, of his frustration, fear and shame, of his loneliness. She poured all the love she had in her soul into her kisses to fill him instead with happiness and pride, joy and satisfaction.

Finally he lifted his head, dragging a breath into

his lungs. She did too, leaning against him with her whole weight, relishing the strength in his powerful frame. 'I love you, Addie.' The words came out raw and ragged. 'Everything I have is yours. Please put me out of my misery. Your kisses say you'll marry me, but…' His eyes blazed down into hers. 'I need to hear it.'

'You've come home, Flynn,' she promised. 'I love you. You're mine and I'm yours. Yes, I'll marry you.'

She watched as the shadows faded from his eyes. 'Home?' he said.

Arm in arm they turned to survey the rolling fields. 'Home,' she repeated, 'because everything I have is yours too, Flynn, and I mean you to have the very best of it.'

'The very best of it is here in my arms.'

'Right answer.' She stretched up on tiptoe to kiss him. His arms snaked about her waist. 'Would you like to go for that gallop now or would you prefer to come up to the house for that, uh…cuppa?'

He grinned. 'The cuppa.'

Taking his hand, she led him back towards the homestead. She led him into the future he'd chosen. She took him home.

* * * * *